If I Forget, You Remember

CAROL LYNCH WILLIAMS

A Yearling Book

Published by
Bantam Doubleday Dell Books for Young Readers
a division of
Random House, Inc.
1540 Broadway
New York, New York 10036

Visit us on the Web! www.randomhouse.com
Educators and librarians, for a variety of teaching tools,
visit us at www.randomhouse.com/teachers

ISBN: 0-440-41420-2

Reprinted by arrangement with Delacorte Press

Printed in the United States of America

July 1999

10 9 8 7 6 5

OPM

to Vickie Finlay Keene—
and I won't forget . . .
I hope

Chapter One

I watched the fat black minute hand jerk toward the one. We had two minutes left in class now and I dreaded the thought that school would be out for the summer. Not because I didn't want a vacation. That wasn't it at all. I knew I was going to miss Mrs. Earl's creative writing class. Utah studies, science, beginning soccer, prealgebra and art were classes I could do without for a few months. Okay, maybe I'd still like to be in art. I really like color even though I'm not that good at drawing. But I would miss creative writing for sure. A lump came up in my throat just thinking about it.

Mr. Blandford had lost control of Utah studies. In fact, he had joined in throwing paper airplanes and was chanting "Alaska . . . Alaska" with a couple of kids.

That's where he's going to be spending the summer. Taking pictures on America's Last Frontier.

An airplane shot through the air and stuck in my shoulder-length hair. I wasn't sure who'd thrown it.

"Come on, Elyse," Anna-Leigh shouted at me from the other side of the room. "Help with the count-down." Anna-Leigh is pretty except for her fat. She's really big. But everyone still seems to like her. Maybe it's because last year she sat on one of the school bullies and pounded him in the back with her fists until our principal, Mr. Brinkerhoff, came and hefted her up. Mr. Brinkerhoff is as big as she is so he didn't have any real trouble pulling Anna-Leigh to her feet. You gotta have a lot of respect for someone who knocks down a major problem in the hall at school, right near the cafeteria, then beats the breath out of him. I sure do.

I stood and let the airplane ride in my hair to where Anna-Leigh was, her large arms circling two thin kids. Maybe they looked thin because Anna-Leigh was in between them. One was Sara Bailey, a jock-type girl who always wins whatever game she plays. The other person was Bruce A. The A. stands for Aufhammer but he's been called Bruce A. since I can remember because we have two Bruces in class. Bruce A. and Bruce R. As a matter of fact, I'm not too sure what Bruce

R.'s last name is because it's so weird. Maybe Rumpel-
stiltskin.

Anyway, Bruce A. waved me over and when I got
close to him he slung his arm onto my shoulder. Just
like that. Thump, his arm was on my shoulder. It
made it kind of hard to breathe. Not because his arm is
heavy or anything. It's because I've had a crush on him
since he read out loud, in Mrs. Earl's class, a science
fiction story he wrote.

"Count," he commanded. And I did. I counted
away the last ten seconds of sixth grade. "Ten, nine,
eight . . ." Maybe if I slowed way down . . .
"Seven, six, five," I shouted after everyone else.
"Four." . . . "Four." . . . I was never going to
have Mrs. Earl as a teacher again. "Three." . . .
"Three." Bruce A. looked at me funny. I noticed his
breath smelled like old pizza. "Two." . . . "Two."
My crush was gone. I wanted his arm off me. "One."
. . . "One."

The bell didn't ring. The tall black hand stood
straight up, pointing right on the twelve, and quivered.
But the bell didn't ring.

Bruce A. turned and looked at me. "What'd ya do
to it, Donaldson?" His eyes were very blue, with
specks of gold right close to the black parts. My crush
was back again. So what's a little pizza breath?

I started to say, "I bewitched the clock. School will never get out," when the bell jangled, loud.

"You're free!" Mr. Blandford shouted; then he raced out of the room ahead of everyone else.

Bruce A. dropped his arm and hugged Anna-Leigh. I noticed his hands didn't quite meet in the back.

I went to my desk and gathered my school stuff. Everyone was running for the door. Pushing, shoving, popping through and out to freedom.

I put my backpack up onto my shoulder. It was light because we had turned in all our books two days before.

"Good-bye, Donaldson," Bruce A. called.

"Yeah, good-bye, Elyse," Anna-Leigh said.

I waved to them and to a few other kids who were calling good-bye to me and started off for Mrs. Earl's class. I wanted to see her one last time. She was in her room, standing at her file cabinet, sorting through papers.

"Mrs. Earl," I said, and she turned around.

"Oh, Elyse," she said. That's one thing about Mrs. Earl. She always sounds like she's glad to see you. "Are you ready for vacation?"

I nodded, even though it was a kind-of lie. You know, not quite true, not quite a lie.

"Any plans?"

"Not really," I said. And that was a kind-of lie, too.

I planned to write a book. I wasn't sure what about yet, but I knew I was going to write one. I was a little embarrassed to tell anyone my plans, even Mrs. Earl.

Mrs. Earl walked over to where I stood leaning on the pale green doorjamb. "Whatever you do," she said, "don't stop writing." She smiled at me. Her braces were done with pink bands this month. I was happy to see that none of the cafeteria pizza was sticking in her teeth. Not that there ever was any. "You're a world-class writer," Mrs. Earl said. "I'd like to think that another Emily Dickinson was born right here." She motioned to her classroom.

I felt kind of stunned that she said I had talent. At first all I could do was blink. Then I managed to say, "All right. I will keep on writing. Maybe I'll even do a novel." I let her in on my secret. *Talent,* I thought. *She said I have talent.* It wasn't something that Mrs. Earl said to any old body. In fact, mostly she said things like "Interesting" or "I've never read anything quite like this." The only person I ever heard her say had any talent was Bruce A. That was the day I got my crush on him. Now I was ranked up there *with* him.

"A novel's a good idea," she said. "If that's really what you want to do. Have a good summer, Elyse."

"I will," I said.

"And come and visit me next year."

"Okay." I walked down the quiet hall toward the

glass doors that would set me free for the summer. There was a lump in my throat. Why couldn't every teacher in the whole wide world be as great as Mrs. Earl?

It was hot out after the air-conditioned school. There wasn't a drop of wind. The sky was bright blue and cloudless. In the distance Mount Timpanogos stood huge and snowcapped. I could see a glint of light reflecting from something at nearly the top of the mountain. I knew it was a little shed. Mom and Dad had hiked there when they were first married. Mom told me so.

If Dad hadn't died, I thought, walking down the side-walk that butted up against Eighth North, *I bet he would have hiked up there with me, too. Maybe with the whole family even.*

My dad's been dead for a long time. I hardly ever used to think about him, but lately I have, though I'm not too sure why. There're a few good things about having a father who's been gone for as long as my dad has been.

First, you don't really miss him. You just miss the idea of him. It's not like when Brian Moss's father was killed in a car accident last year. He's still sad about that. And second, you can make up your own memories, all good if you're anything like me.

I looked at the snow up on Timp and wondered

how long it would be before it all melted away. Some summers the snow lingers, growing thin until there's only a long finger of white left, like a streak of paint. That happens when summer is short and fall blows in early and cold. Sometimes the snow melts clean away, and the mountain turns first green with spring and new life, and then brown with the heat. I crossed my fingers for a really hot summer. Then I glanced down the road toward home.

"Oh no," I said, seeing the two kids on bikes. I gulped in a gasp of warm May air and my stomach lurched.

Chapter Two

"**D**on't worry," I said aloud to myself. "You're almost home." But I wasn't really. I had almost a block to go before I'd be safe. I ran across Seventh West, the street that bordered the school soccer field. A few minutes ago the sprinklers had gone off. Seagulls swooped and screamed, hollering to each other about the dinner of worms that was coming to the surface of the soggy field.

The kids on the bikes were close now. I knew them from prealgebra. Patrick Powers and Caleb Norris. Patrick is the bully Anna-Leigh sat on last year because he and Caleb had been calling her really rotten names. I tried to walk faster like I wasn't trying to walk faster.

"Once you get to the corner and turn," I said,

"you'll be able to see home." I could almost make out the rosebushes that poked through Mr. Clark's fence, splashes of bright pink, yellow, white and red. If I could only reach the flowers without getting caught.

They rode by fast on their bikes. I pretended not to notice. Patrick, whose hair is blond like a hot sun, screamed out, "Butthead!" Caleb, whose face began to break out bad as soon as we all stepped into sixth grade, got off his bike and scooped up a handful of gravel from the road. Out of the corner of my eye I saw him straighten. I kept walking, waiting for him to throw. A second later he did. The dirt stung my arms but I didn't look at either one of them. I didn't flinch. Instead I began to sing and march.

"O beau-tee-ful, for spacious skies," I sang as loud as I could. My old beat-up tennis shoes pounded out a rhythm on the sidewalk. Patrick circled back toward me. Caleb got on his bike to follow.

"For amber waves of grain."

"You stupid butthead," Patrick shouted, swooping near like one of the seagulls. He hit me with the handlebar of his mountain bike. It hurt but I kept on going. I made sure my marching steps were large ones.

"You are so crazy," Caleb said. His voice was a sneer.

"For purple mountain's . . ." I was at Mr. Clark's

house now, but I didn't look to the left or the right, just made the turn toward home. *". . . majesty."*

"And ugly," said Patrick.

As if you're telling me something I don't already know, I thought, but I didn't break up the song. *"Above the fruited plain."* I passed the flowers that sent soft smells out to me, not seeing them.

Ahead was my house, light green, a half block from where I was. Something hit my ear. Another pebble. A shower of school papers exploded close by like a small snowstorm. They floated with a whisper to the earth.

"America, America . . ." One of the guys pulled his bike up behind me on the sidewalk. The tire hit me on the heel, pulling my shoe off. I could see the quaking aspen tree in my front yard. *". . . God shed his grace on thee . . ."*

And to my surprise, there stood Jordyn in our driveway. She walked down the sidewalk toward us. I could see that she was mad. I felt like boo-hooing right then and there. Seeing her, I tried not to let any relief cross my face.

"Leave my sister alone," said Jordyn in a loud voice. Her pretty blond hair shone in the sun. Who would think she'd come to my rescue? We haven't been friends since before I was born.

"What are you going to do about it?" Patrick asked, but for some reason he backed off, even

10

though Jordyn is smaller than I am. Laughing, he and Caleb pedaled off together, calling me names. Right then I realized that both those jerks liked my sister. Gross.

I reached for my shoe, and at the top of my lungs I finished the song. *"And crown thy good with brotherhood from sea to shining sea."* I ended with an ear-piercing yodel, my arms stretched out wide like I was going to hug someone. Then I bowed low, letting my fingertips graze against the sidewalk. It was rough to the touch.

Jordyn grabbed hold of my arm and pulled me up straight.

"Thank you, thank you," I said, flinging kisses at imaginary people who were all applauders and not stone throwers.

She steered me toward the house, past our white picket fence with the broken gate. She opened the front door with her free hand and nearly pushed me down trying to get me inside. A burst of cool air greeted me. When the door slammed shut behind us, Jordyn jerked me around to face her.

"What is wrong with you, Elyse?" she yelled. Her breath smelled like peanut butter.

"What do you mean, what's wrong with me?" My hands were shaking, my ear was stinging and I still felt like crying my eyeballs out.

"Why were you letting those two harass you like that?" Jordyn's face was red.

I took in a surprised breath. Hadn't she seen what had happened? Hadn't she seen any of it?

"I wasn't letting them harass me," I said between clenched teeth.

"I watched it all from the living room." Jordyn gestured to the large glass window that let in the hot summer sun.

"If you watched it, Jordyn, then you know what happened."

"You didn't even try to get away. You didn't even run from them." Jordyn's voice was loud.

"You think I can outrun two kids on bicycles?" I said, almost shouting back at her. "I wasn't *letting* them do anything. They were doing it on their own. Like they have nearly every day of my life."

"This is amazing." Jordyn's voice was high with disbelief.

I shrugged and pushed past my sister and on into the living room. I needed to sit down. My legs were shaking.

Jordyn followed, her hands on her hips. "So why haven't you ever knocked that stupid Powers kid off his bike and onto his butt?"

"Are you kidding, Jordyn?" I asked, surprised that

my straight-A sister would even say something like that. "And have him squash my face flat?"

"Right, Elyse. Those guys wouldn't hurt you."

I got mad then. "You don't even know either one of them. I've had bruises where they've hit me before. If I knocked one of them off his bike, they'd both try to kill me."

Jordyn's face got a funny look on it.

"So why haven't you told Mom?"

"I can't," I said. The lump in my throat grew fatter and I found myself feeling sorry about my sad life. "Mom has enough to worry about without me doing a song and dance for her."

"You mean like the one you did for those two jackasses?" Jordyn started to grin. Instead she made her face straight and said, "I thought they only *said* stuff. When did they start hurting you?"

For some reason her words bothered me. My voice came out snottier than I meant. "The words hurt, too, Miss Perfect. As if you would even know. Everyone likes you."

"Geez, Elyse," Jordyn said, her face hard again. "I don't know why I even try to talk to you."

"I'm sorry," I said.

But Jordyn stomped off to her room. I didn't follow her, even though I wanted to say thank you. Instead I

13

whispered it at her door. "Thanks for saving me, Big Sis."

Then I started humming "America." I made up a verse thanking Mrs. Emery, my fourth-grade teacher, for teaching my class the words to the song. It was a lifesaver.

Chapter Three

Private Journal of Elyse Donaldson, World-class Writer. Ideas so far: Gorillas, cats, bullies, summer vacation My list for what I can write about isn't going so good, let me tell you.

purple mountain's majesty

The next morning I was sitting at my desk getting ready to write a book when Mom came to the doorway.

"Elyse," she said, and her voice sounded real quiet.

Uh-oh, I thought. There was something about Mom's voice that meant trouble. I sat still. Maybe if I didn't move she wouldn't see me because of all my stuff. Like a chameleon or something.

Chameleon is a novel idea, I thought, but I didn't say anything, just tried to hide. My desk was covered with my writing paper and crayons. I had gotten this great idea to do each chapter in a different color. A white wicker-framed mirror hung right where I could see myself when I wrote. That way I could make all kinds of expressions in the mirror, see what they really looked like and then describe them. Mrs. Earl always says description is important.

Granddaddy and Granny's picture, the last one taken before Granddaddy's heart attack, was propped near the mirror. There was also a picture of my dad and me. The picture was a little blurry. Dad was standing there holding me in his arms, grinning. His hair was just as dark as mine is now. I had pasted a little heart-shaped sticker onto the glass that said I Love You.

"Elyse," Mom said again. "Your room."

"Yes, Mom?" I asked, acting like I suddenly heard her. Mom had pulled her long blond hair into a house-cleaning ponytail. Today was house-cleaning day. Every Saturday of my life is house-cleaning day.

"This is the first Saturday of vacation, Mom," I said when she ignored my pretending not to know what was going on. "And anyway, I'm writing a book."

Mom looked bugged. "Let's not talk about writing. Let's talk about this room."

"Mom," I said. "It's not even ten yet. Ten A.M., Mom. Morning. You know how I do in the morning." I am definitely a night person. I can hardly take a step in the morning, much less clean.

"I know what time it is," Mom said. "It's time for you to get going. You have chores. Jordyn is done with her room."

"Jordyn's room was done before she even began."

With my luck Jordyn was probably cleaning out the attic right this very minute, to get on Mom's good side. She always does everything Mom wants her to do. Mom thinks Jordyn is an angel, and I guess she is, but it bothers me half to death. Every time I turn around my sister is right there showing how wonderful she is. At home, at school, in sports, everywhere. It's disgusting. Sometimes I hate her guts.

"Elyse, take a look at this room."

I looked around.

My bed was unmade. Stuffed animals were all over the floor, along with all my clothes, clean and dirty. There were papers everywhere, beginnings of stories that weren't quite right. Crayons that didn't make good chapter colors were on the floor too. There was underwear, a clean pair I was sure, hanging on the curtain rod. I'd have to remember that the next time I ran out.

Dirty glasses lined the windowsill. Game pieces to Monopoly and Clue, and Uno cards, were dumped in front of the closet, along with three sweaters, my snow boots and my favorite ski jacket, which was two inches too short for me in the arms. I was thinking of making a vest out of it. Of course I don't sew very well, but I am pretty handy using a glue gun. The only neat thing about my room was my bookshelf. All my books were stacked in piles around it, in the order I wanted to read them this summer.

My life was a great big pile. I liked it that way.

"So?" I asked.

Mom closed her eyes.

"So? So clean it." Mom was not in a mood to be played with. I could tell by her tone. After a second her voice softened. "Look, I'll make a deal with you."

I turned in my chair and looked at Mom. The change in her voice was one I hadn't heard in a long time. Gentle and not worried. Kind of the way it was before money got tight. Before Mom started working full-time for Dr. Lauret. It made me homesick.

"Clean it today only," she said. "Do it this one day before the summer officially begins and I won't bother you about it again all vacation. Just start the summer off clean."

Mom stood in the doorway, waiting.

I sat there in my straight-backed chair twirling a silver crayon between my fingers. Silver, gold and copper always make great chapter headings. I pretended that I wasn't as excited as heck about what Mom offered me. A whole, entire summer off. No bedroom work for almost three months. A song should be written about this. Luck was looking my way. The sun was shining on me. Life was going to be . . .

"Well?" Mom asked. She sure wasn't being patient.

"Hmmm," I said aloud like I was considering the offer, but inside I said, *Oh yes, oh yes, yes, yes, YES!* "You promise I won't have to do anything in here all summer?"

I could tell that answering took a huge effort on Mom's part. She closed her eyes again and sucked in a deep breath.

"That's the deal," she said, her teeth clenched and her voice even.

"You won't harass me?" To myself I sounded like a lawyer from TV, pushing for the truth.

Mom shook her head, and her cleaning ponytail waved around her shoulders.

"You won't come in to check on me, to see how bad things look in here? You do that a lot, you know. You won't do any eyeball rolling?"

"I said—"

"And you won't—"

"That's it, Elyse. Yes or no?"

I figured I had bugged Mom enough, so I said quick-like, "It's a deal. Today and today only. Should we shake on it?" I started to get up but Mom stopped me with The Look.

I smiled. "Okay, Mom. It's a deal."

Mom turned and started away. "Please get it done as soon as possible, all right, Elyse? And, honey, take the glasses down to the dishwasher. No wonder we always run short of things to drink out of."

Mom's voice sounded so nice that I was struck by a pang of guilt right in the center of my guts. I felt a sudden rush of love for her. Why did I torture her so much? "I'll do a super-good job," I called, thinking that I might even clean under the bed.

Jordyn poked her head into my room. " 'I'll do a super-good job,' " she mimicked. Then she looked around the room. "What a pigsty. You're going to need a dump truck to get rid of the junk in here."

I was angry immediately. "Get out of here before I punch you in your big fat ugly nose," I said. Jordyn's nose is perfect, really, but she's always standing in the bathroom wishing she can get a nose job because she's so self-conscious about it. I try and help her out with her nose self-esteem anytime I can.

"Ooooh, I'm sooo scared," Jordyn said, but she ran down the hall when I stood up. Boy, could she ever bug me. It made me think that maybe I had imagined her defending me yesterday.

Not only does Jordyn bug me half to death, but she's the pretty one in the family, too. You'd think having Mom's blue eyes and small build would be enough for her to leave me alone. She's always teasing me about my size, about my room, about my ugly teeth, about how boys will never call me. Here she is, only fourteen, and boys from school are always calling her. They have been for years, it seems.

As if I even want them to call me. Well, maybe Bruce A. But I sure wouldn't want to go do anything with him. You know, like date, or kiss. Yuck!

It isn't easy being stuck looking exactly like my father. I don't want to be as tall as a house, with feet huge enough to snow-ski on without skis and arms so long I sometimes expect my knuckles to drag on the ground. I don't want plain old brown eyes and very straight light brown hair. I don't want to have to wear braces.

I should have punched Jordyn a good one, even if she did help me out yesterday. Right in her pretty little turned-up nose.

Bam! I thought. *Splat!*

I faked a punch at the wall. With a sigh I pushed away from my desk and started cleaning. I worked right through lunch. I left my room only to make deliveries. One delivery was when I took all my clothes, clean and dirty, to the laundry room. The others were when I took my assorted glass collection to the kitchen. I made quite a few trips with that. I had been able to get fifteen glasses onto my windowsill before Mom had asked for them.

I know girls at school who have collections of tiny animals and other figurines. I've never really seen them but I've heard kids talking about them. In fact, this one girl, Kathy, all she ever does is brag about what she's gotten from her daddy, who shops in foreign countries. Once, when she was standing in a circle of her friends, close-like to my desk, they all turned to me.

"Do you collect anything, Elyse Donaldson?" she asked. Some of the girls giggled. One couldn't even look me in the eye, she was laughing so hard.

"Yeah," I said, wanting really bad to join their circle and knowing it would never happen. "I collect something."

"Oh?" Kathy asked. "What?" She sounded genuinely surprised that I'd do anything that might be considered girly.

"I collect boogers. Hard and soft. Got any to donate?"

I didn't get any popularity awards that year in school. In fact, my little story made it back to Jordyn, who yelled all over the house that I was so stupid she was ashamed to be anyplace I was. She wanted to have me transferred to the private school in the next town so I wouldn't embarrass her anymore.

I felt awful that whole day. I couldn't wait for the hollering to stop so I could call Granny. We're pretty good friends. I tell her stuff that's going on, like Caleb and Patrick and if I get good grades or not. I've even told her my dream to be a writer. She's the only one in the family who knows.

Anyway, here it was a year later and my booger lie still haunted me, but it was usually some boy laughing about how, for the first time in all our years at school, Kathy Keene hadn't had anything to say to anybody. And the story gets bigger and bigger. In fact, the last time I heard it told, one kid said somebody threw up because I showed the boogers right there in Mrs. Rogers's fifth-grade class. But that part is not true.

I thought about all this while I cleaned my room and sent my only collection off to take a ride through the dishwasher. By dinner my room was clean, except under the bed, and I was ready for a work-free, writing-filled summer. Life had never looked so good. That evening, after reading some of *The Long Winter,* I set a milk glass on the windowsill to start all over again. The summer was mine.

Chapter Four

*Private Journal of Elyse Donaldson: World-class Writer.
Ideas so far: My own version of* Stuart Little   *I
know I should be working on an original idea, but think of
this: Stuart is a girl instead of a boy—named Alicia. Dog
instead of cat is the enemy, does ballet*

wild watermelon

At eleven o'clock that night Mom came in to tell
me she was going to bed. I could tell she was
trying hard not to roll her eyes and mumble "How in
the world did you get your room messy so fast?"
Really, things weren't that bad . . . yet.

"Un-lax, Mom," I said, using a word Granny says
whenever I'm worried about something.

"I wish you could understand my position, Elyse,"
Mom said. I could tell by her voice that she was tired. I
felt a stab of guilt. "It's hard doing this alone."

"I'm trying," I said, and I meant it.

"Thank you, honey," Mom said, and she came in
and sat on the side of the bed. "You did work hard
today. And I appreciate it. Don't stay up too late."

"Okay, and you're welcome." I had already decided

to stay up all night reading, so I didn't quite look Mom in the eye when I answered her. Mom left and I was a few chapters into *Maniac Magee* when Jordyn went by and snorted like a pig. I pretended she actually looked like a pig. I couldn't help but grin at her turning in a huff when I called, "Sooo-eeeey!" at her.

At two A.M. I had just finished *Maniac* when the phone rang. I was so involved with my reading that I actually jumped. I threw back the covers and ran down the hall on my tiptoes, to the kitchen. Who could be calling this late at night?

"Hello?" I said, keeping my voice low. I didn't want to wake up Mom. Maybe it was that guy with the magazines and stamps calling to say I'd won a million dollars. Or somebody who wanted to make my future novel into a movie.

Someone was whispering. I wanted it to be the million-dollar guy so much that at first I thought it *was* him. But why would he whisper?

"Killers," the voice said. A cold feeling crept into the pit of my stomach. This was not the prize guy. I almost hung up but then I recognized Granny's voice.

"Granny?" I asked. "Is that you?"

"Hush," Granny said. "I don't want anyone to know I'm calling you."

"What?"

"I said, 'Hush.' "

"Okay," I whispered.

"Listen carefully," she continued. "A band of robbers, at this very moment, is circling my apartment. Every once in a while I hear them tapping on the window. They have guns and ice picks. I'm caught in a dilemma. Should I shoot them dead in their tracks? Or offer them coffee with poison in it?"

"Granny," I asked, "is this a joke?"

"No," Granny said. "I am dead serious. And since it is pretty serious to be dead I need you to help me."

"Calm down," I said, my heart thumping loud. "No one is running around *your* apartment. You live on the third floor."

"Then they're jumping real hard. I'm telling you, Addie, I've looked out the window one hundred times if I've looked out once, and each time I see a dirty old man looking in at me."

"Granny, this is Elyse."

"Who?" Granny seemed really surprised, like I *should* be Addie.

"Me. Elyse. Your granddaughter."

"I've dialed the wrong number. Who'd you say you are?"

"Elyse Donaldson, Granny."

"I haven't called Addie Webster?"

"No ma'am. You've reached your daughter's house. And this is your granddaughter."

Granny was quiet; then she said, "But what about that dirty old man? I tell you I've seen an old man staring in at me every time I look out the window." Granny sounded like she was getting scared.

"Don't worry," I said. "I think you're seeing your reflection in the window. There's no way an old man could climb up your apartment building wall, not even if he had Spider-Man suction cups on his hands and feet."

Granny took in a deep breath. When she spoke I knew she wasn't scared anymore. She was just plain angry.

"Addie, you can rot in hell. I am no one's granny, as you say. I am as young as you are. In the prime of my life and you know it. You're saying those nasty things because I won Miss Strawberry Days and you didn't." Granny slammed down the receiver. There was silence.

I stood in the dark kitchen holding the phone. The light from my room lit up a square of gray carpeting. Mom came walking through it, bright for a moment in her old beat-up housecoat, to where I was.

"Granny?" she asked.

I nodded. "How did you know?" I hung up the phone in its cradle and stood there, shaking in the warmth of a summer night. My grandmother had scared me.

"She's been calling a lot lately." Mom stood with

her arms across her chest for a minute, then asked, "Care to share a snack with me?" She didn't wait for an answer but came into the kitchen. She turned on the light over the stove and then started pulling things out of the fridge: chicken left over from dinner, potato salad, biscuits.

"What's wrong with her?" I asked Mom when we sat in the semidark room at our green Formica table. "Why isn't she asleep? And why did she call me Addie? Did she mean Great-aunt Addie?"

Mom shrugged her shoulders.

"I don't know, honey. Maybe there was something in your voice that reminded her of her sister," she said. "Or maybe Granny was thinking of Aunt Addie before she picked up the phone."

"Weird," I said. "Aunt Addie's been dead forever."

Mom was silent a second. "She's been calling a lot and I'm worried."

"Who, Aunt Addie?" I asked, trying to be funny.

"No, your grandmother."

The cold feeling was back in my stomach.

"She's going to die, isn't she?" I asked. First Dad, then Granddaddy and now Granny.

"Well, Elyse, she is almost seventy. I don't expect her to keep living forever. But I'm worried about the way she's acting. You know she has Alzheimer's."

"Kind of," I said. "I remember you talking about it a long time ago. Why hasn't it gotten better yet?" It seemed the last time I had heard about Alzheimer's was when Granddaddy was alive.

Mom took a bite of potato salad and chewed like she was thinking. "Well, it's a forgetting disease that never goes away."

"Then I've got it." I always lose things. Mom says if I kept my room straightened then I could find my stuff when I want it.

Mom kind of laughed. "No, it's a different kind of forgetting. It's permanent. It begins small with people losing things like their keys."

I *was* getting Alzheimer's. This was my mother's kind way of letting me know how sick I was. My stomach started hurting.

"Then it gets bigger. Granny is past just forgetting," Mom said. "She's losing her 'now' memories."

"What's a now memory?"

"Well, it's her present. The things that she's living through. With Alzheimer's you lose your memory from the now to the past."

I felt confused. I usually couldn't remember things from a long time ago.

"For example, Granny not knowing who you were. Sometimes she doesn't know who *I* am."

I guess I didn't have Alzheimer's after all. I know

Mom pretty darn well. And I couldn't imagine anyone not remembering their own kid.

"She gets lost really easy."

Well, if there is one thing I am good at, it's finding my way around. Mom says I could be a mapmaker, I'm so good at remembering where we've been.

Mom seemed to be almost talking to herself, thinking about Granny. "Eventually there won't be anything of her memory left. I'm not real sure what to do. There's always a convalescent center."

I stopped dreaming about mapmaking as a career. "I don't think Granny would like to do that, Mom," I said. "She likes living on her own. Remember when you and Aunt Maggie moved Granny and Granddaddy from their place in Lindon? She chewed the two of you out over that for a long time. And she still talks about her old house."

Mom sipped at a glass of milk. "I feel guilty about that even now. Granddaddy's dying was so unexpected. I thought they'd help him take care of Granny there, what with a nurse and aides on duty all the time."

"What do you mean?" I asked. "I didn't know Granddaddy was taking care of Granny."

Mom sighed. "Oh, Elyse, this has been going on for a couple of years. And you know how Granddaddy was. He never minded helping Granny. He sure did love her. Even when she began to . . ." Mom paused. ". . . change." She stopped talking, remembering her parents.

After a minute Mom said, "Granny made me promise never to put her in an old folks' home. She's always thought they're sad and lonely. And since we're on the subject, I'm gonna make you promise me the same thing." Mom pointed at me with her fork. "When and if the time comes, put me in a big hole in the backyard, lock me in the basement or store me in the attic. But whatever you do, don't leave me to waste away in one of those places." She shivered. "I used to work in a convalescent center. I was a nurse's aide."

"Oh yeah?" I asked. "When?" The chicken was good cold if you pulled off the lumpy skin.

"Right before I met your father. I stayed there even after we got married. I worked at Annie's Retirement Home until I got pregnant with Jordyn. It was a sad place."

"So why did you stay?"

"To keep those people from being lonely. I stayed because lots of the old folks needed a friend." Mom sighed again and then she ate in silence. I sat quiet, eating too. That sounded like my Mom, all right,

31

working someplace only because she thought she might help someone. I'll never do that. When I get old enough to get a job, it'll be exactly what I want to do. I'll be a writer. And I won't stick around Utah, either. I'll go to a faraway island to do my work.

As we straightened up the kitchen to go back to bed I asked Mom, "So what are the chances of Alzheimer's for me? I mean, you know I'm always losing things. But not myself. I don't lose myself at all."

Mom smiled. "You're safe, Elyse. Alzheimer's is a disease that most often affects older people." Mom paused then and looked out the kitchen window and into our dark backyard. "Poor Granny. She never thought this would happen to her. You know, that she'd get old like this."

"Poor Granny," I said, agreeing with Mom, feeling lots better now that I knew that Granny wasn't ready to die at any moment and I didn't have Alzheimer's.

"Elyse," Mom said. She had moved to the table and was wiping it clean. She tightened her housecoat around her small waist, then smoothed back her hair with one hand. "I've been thinking about asking her to come live with us. I've talked with Maggie a bit already, and she agrees something different has to be done." Mom paused to see how I would take this. I let the words have a chance to sink in and said nothing.

"If I can get up the nerve, I'll drop the bomb on her when she comes to dinner this week."

I thought about Granny maybe living with us. I kind of liked the idea. I wouldn't have to call her when I needed to talk to her about a problem. She'd already be here.

"It's okay by me," I said. "Granny could share my room."

Mom didn't say anything, but she did look at me hard. "I still have a few days to work out any kinks. I'll think about it at work." She's an assistant at a dentist's office. She always comes home smelling very fresh, like the stuff they put on your teeth when you get them cleaned.

I shrugged. "Okay," I said. "Do I get to keep the no-cleaning-my-room-all-summer bargain no matter if I share with Granny?"

Mom sort of chuckled and I was glad because she didn't seem so upset anymore. "I made a deal," she said. "I'll remember my promise. I don't think you'll have to share a room with anybody, though."

Hmmm, I thought. *I won't have to share with anybody? Where in the world would we get the room to have an extra person with her own room?* But I didn't say anything.

Mom stood at the table, looking into the darkness of our shabby front room. After a little bit she said, "The scary thing is that we're all gonna get old."

"Not me," I said. "I'm gonna live forever at the perfect age."

"And what age is that, Miss Elyse?" Mom asked.

"I don't know," I said. "But I am sure it's not twelve."

Mom laughed, then kissed me hard on the forehead.

Chapter Five

Private Journal of Elyse Donaldson, World-class Writer.
Ideas so far: Goats, the underworld, keeping a clean house
Will Granny stay here?

olive green

Mom always left early for Provo, where Dr. Lauret's office is. She'd come in, dressed in the pink-and-blue-plaid shirt that's the office uniform, and kiss me good-bye. Sometimes I'd wake up. Sometimes not. The times I didn't get up, I missed my mom all day.

That's what happened the next morning. I missed Mom. That started the whole day off wrong. I kept dreaming about a giant bee that buzzed around my room. Mrs. Earl, wearing a purple leotard and a green tutu, rode the bee near the ceiling. Every once in a while she'd shout, "Seen my keys?" In my dream I searched through a dirty bedroom.

The buzzing finally woke me up. It was the vacuum cleaner.

Here I'd planned a perfect summer of reading and sleeping and it would never happen. I mean, Jordyn was around. Vacuuming right outside my bedroom door. I'm sure she did it on purpose, trying to get me up early because she likes to get up at the crack of dawn. She stood there in the doorway, vacuuming until I thought she had sucked all the carpet threads from that one spot.

I gave her the evil eye and was able to get back to sleep, but only for a little while because then Jordyn started jumping around the living room to an exercise videotape she has. Suddenly last summer came barging into my dreams. Every day had been the same: Jordyn up early, doing her chores; Jordyn exercising with some super-skinny lady in a very tiny bathing suit; Jordyn taking extra-loud (her singing) and -long (no hot water when she's done) showers. I felt a pain behind my eyes that came with the thought of what would happen to me for another summer.

"Hey, string bean," I yelled when I wandered in for breakfast. Jordyn had moved the coffee table and was kicking around the living room, causing the lampshades to shake. "Why don't you turn down the sound?" I marched over in my sweats (I sleep in sweats regardless of the weather, winter or summer) and turned the sound completely off. The skinny lady in the tiny bathing suit jumped around on a beach. An old lady, a fat lady and two men exercised with her. Jordyn kicked in my direction, just missing me. "Careful, beanie," I said. "Or I'll snap you in two." I felt good about my little joke. "Get it? String *bean*. I'll *snap* you in two."

Jordyn ignored me. I hate it when she does that, and she knows it. Breakfast could wait. I decided to exercise with her. I flailed my arms around, smacking Jordyn every third or fourth flail.

"One, two, three, four," I shouted. "Make your fat shake out the door. Five, six, seven, eight. You're never gonna lose that weight. Now jiggle, jiggle. Make your butt wiggle." I hit Jordyn a good one in the ear.

"You jerk," Jordyn shouted. "I hate you." To my surprise she started crying and ran from the room.

Well, that was a first. Jordyn never cries, at least not where I can see her. I felt a pang of guilt but squished it flat right away by making fun of the exercising old lady and fat lady. They were stretching out their arms, pointing at me.

"I bet those two are off to McDonald's as soon as this segment of video is over," I said aloud. I turned the TV off, then went into the kitchen and poured myself a bowl of cereal. Okay, for brunch. It was late morning. Stupid Jordyn hadn't woken me as early as I thought.

A few minutes later she came into the kitchen, her eyes and nose red from crying.

"What is wrong with you, Elyse?" she asked, her voice hot with anger. "I've tried and tried to be your friend and you won't have it. Why can't you leave me alone?"

I kept eating, pretending like I didn't feel bad about my sister's red nose. I started humming.

"Don't ignore me," she said. "I know you can hear me. And I know something else, too. I can answer a few of your little questions."

Jordyn waved around a spiral notebook of mine that had KEEP OUT! JOURNAL #6 written in black and gray crayon on the front.

"I've read your stupid diary, written in all those dumb colors."

At first I was so surprised to see my book flapping around that I could barely think. I couldn't move and I even forgot to chew. Of all the journals to get, she had to find the one from school this past year.

" 'I don't understand it,' " Jordyn read, exaggerating her voice and making it all whiny so the words I had written came out childish. " 'I feel terrible. Nobody at school likes me. I want friends but I'm not sure how to get them.' "

"Give me that back," I screamed, spraying

Crunchberries. I lunged for the notebook. Milk dribbled down my chin.

I guess Jordyn's exercises were paying off. Usually I'm faster than she is in short distances and my long arms and legs give me a reach advantage. But this time she danced out of my way, her face splotchy from anger.

"You want an answer, Elyse. It's because you're so mean and selfish. It's because you do dumb things like tell people you collect boogers. You're the booger girl who can think only of herself. Who *could* like you?" Jordyn jabbed at me with one slender finger. Her nail was painted pearly orange.

I felt like I had been punched hard in the stomach. At first I couldn't take in a breath. Then, it seemed, I was full of action. "Give me that back, Rudolph Reindeer," I said, throwing the spoon I held into the bowl and turning to face my sister for the fight.

"You sing the national anthem for attention. You'll always be a loner and you'll always get beat up."

I knew I had been mean to Jordyn, but not *that* mean.

"It wasn't the national anthem," I screamed. "It was 'America.' Don't you know your music? Now give . . . me . . . my . . . book . . . back."

I sprang forward, somehow hitting a chair and

knocking both it and myself to the ground. I landed on my knees and when I did Jordyn hit me hard, twice, on top of the head with my diary. For a brief second I really saw stars. She threw the notebook at my feet and ran.

I caught her in her bedroom. I punched her hard between the shoulder blades. Another first happened then. Jordyn turned to fight me. We wrestled all over her room, silently, even though there wasn't anyone in the house to hear us. We punched and clawed and pulled and poked each other, only making occasional *oomph* sounds. We fought until we were both worn out and I was finally able to hold Jordyn down because I outweighed her. I sat on her stomach and held her hands flat on the floor.

"Give," I said between clenched teeth.

But Jordyn said nothing.

"So I'm stupid," I said. "So what. And I will make friends this summer. You wait and see."

Jordyn looked past my ear like I wasn't there.

My face burned from the fight and from embarrassment at sitting on my tiny older sister and from anger.

I hated it that I didn't get along with Jordyn. I hated it that I was lonely and did badly in school except for art and creative writing. I hated it that I was as big as a horse.

I got up off Jordyn with a sigh.

The summer would be only okay. No, the summer would drag on and on and on. And I was going to have to spend it alone, when I had thought that somehow I might be able to make friends with my sister.

Chapter Six

Private Journal of Elyse Donaldson, World-class Writer.
Ideas so far: Boring summer, no friends, fights, mean-
mean sisters   Nothing is sacred with Jordyn around.
I will have to begin hiding these thoughts in a new place.

cornflower

I got on my bike and headed off for a while. I rode over to the Orem public library. A new addition, with its huge window of stained glass, stood in the grassy area where Dad, Mom, Jordyn and I used to have picnics. But that was a long time ago. I was barely four. Now this part of the library was for kids, the children's wing.

"Someday," I said to no one, "I'll have my own books in there."

I parked my bike and went into the library. The cool air was fresh and felt especially good on the places where sweat had trickled down my face on my ride over. Closing my eyes, I sniffed deep. Books have to be my favorite nonfood smell in the world. After a minute I took the elevator to the children's section, went to a big square table and sat down. I pulled a pad of paper and a pencil out of my backpack and got ready to write a book again. I hadn't had a chance since cleaning day. Working and fighting with Jordyn had taken up all my free time.

I licked the lead of the pencil the way I had seen someone do in the movies and began to write.

Well, I tried to begin to write.

No idea came.

I sat a little longer. I looked at the large green dragon on the ceiling. *Someone is a very good artist,* I thought. The dragon was huge and took up most of the space. I wondered if maybe I couldn't do a little drawing myself. Maybe that would inspire the words.

I tried to sketch the dragon. I made his tail curl around the holes in the paper. He didn't look a thing like the library dragon.

I looked around the room. Hmm, still no idea.

Words. Maybe if I concentrated on one specific idea—like mean sisters. I closed my eyes and thought. I tried to picture Jordyn as the villain in my novel, but the only person who seemed to fit in that place was myself. Never mind that idea after all.

Mrs. Earl said that sometimes ideas would come if you just started writing any old thing. Maybe I should write a letter.

I decided to write the mayor of Orem and thank

him for making the library bigger. I wasn't sure if making the library bigger was just his idea, but I'd be sure to tell him to tell anybody else who helped think it up thanks too.

It only took a couple of minutes to thank the mayor. I took my box of 120 crayons from my backpack and selected blizzard blue for the beginning of the letter. I signed my name in neon carrot. When it was finished I folded the paper carefully and put it in an envelope. I always bring everything I might need for book or letter writing with me. I like being prepared.

Now for my novel. I smiled at the thought of having something published.

"Hey, Donaldson." I jumped at my name. Bruce A. dropped a pile of books onto the table across from me. "Mind if I sit here?" He didn't wait for an answer, just plopped in the chair and started looking through the books he'd carried over. I noticed most of them had to do with small businesses and running newspapers. The one on the bottom of the stack said *Publishing Your Own Newspaper*.

Yuck, I thought, but I said, "Why are you reading all that stuff? School's out, you know."

He smiled at me, a really big smile, and I saw that his two front teeth were a little crooked. I wondered if my orthodontist could make my teeth look like that. Just a little crooked.

"It's my dad," Bruce A. said.

"What's your dad?" I glanced around the library. There was only one man here with us and that was the librarian.

"My dad's not here," Bruce A. said. "He's the reason *I'm* here. He doesn't want me sitting around all day long during the summer. So he told me to start a business and he'd help pay for it. You know. For the experience."

"Yeah," I said, though I really didn't know. "So . . ."

"So I've decided to start a newspaper for our neighborhood."

"Oh."

We both sat quiet; then Bruce A. opened a book and started reading.

I peeked at him whenever I was sure he wasn't looking at me. His skin was already tanned brown. He had on a T-shirt and I could see a real bad scrape on his arm. Thank goodness he wasn't picking at it. I really hate that kind of thing. You know, picking.

His hair was wavy and almost the color of my burnt sienna crayon, with some blond and red too.

He looked up and caught me staring at him.

"What?" I asked, a little too loud.

"What what?" he said, and he smiled again.

I felt my face grow hot. I was probably the real, true

45

red color. Can't get any more blushed-looking than that.

"What did you do to your arm?" It was the only thing I could think to say.

"I was rappelling with my dad. My line slipped a little and I did this." He pointed to his arm. "Could have been worse."

I felt my lip raise a little at the thought of his having more scabs than he already had. Try as I might, I couldn't get the sneer to go away.

"Hmm" was all I could say. I decided not to go climbing any mountains.

"What're you doing this summer?" he asked.

Sweat broke out on my upper lip. Was he going to ask me on a date thing? No, that couldn't be. He'd asked about the summer.

Having him look at me that way made it hard to talk. "The summer? I'll, uh, be writing, I think."

"Oh yeah?" Bruce A. seemed interested. He raised his eyebrows, blond and tan colored. "What?"

I blinked. "I'm not too sure. A novel, I think." My secret was out and a near stranger had pried it from me.

Bruce A. nodded. "Listen, Donaldson," he said, leaning toward me. His lips were very pink, almost the wild strawberry color. "I'm going to need a couple of people to help me with the paper this summer.

Anna-Leigh will be doing the artwork. But I need some writers. I thought you and me. Of course we'll use my computer, but there might be some cutting and pasting, and we could all work on that together."

"What?" I could still feel the sneer. Was it going to stay there forever? "What's cutting and pasting? Kindergarten stuff?"

Bruce A. smiled. "That's when you move a picture or something at the last minute, only you do it by hand. At school we did most of the layout on the computer. Or on a lightboard. But I don't have one at home."

"Oh," I said, like I knew what a lightboard was. I was concentrating on making the sneer disappear from my face, so I hardly heard a thing Bruce A. was saying. *Smile,* I kept telling myself. *Smile.*

". . . come over and help," Bruce A. finished.

"Excuse me?" I asked. Had he asked me over? My hands began to sweat.

"I said Anna-Leigh and I could use your help. I was wondering if you'd like to work on the paper with us. It'd mean going out and getting stories."

"Sure," I said. "I'll help." A chance to write! A deadline might actually help me get going.

"I couldn't pay you anything. This will be a free paper."

I nodded.

"Okay. We're starting tomorrow. You know where I live, right? The big blue house a few streets over from you."

"Yeah, I know," I said. How could I not know? Bruce A. comes from a very large Mormon family. There are ten kids and he's about third or fourth from the top. His house is huge because every time another kid gets born, Mr. A. builds on another room. So they have this big old house, with a tall pointy roof. Some of the kids from over at the Mormon church have even practiced rappelling down the back. Mr. A. helps and everything.

"Okay. Be there around eleven. Just come on over. And bring any ideas for what we can write about."

Oh great, I thought. I had trouble finding ideas for my own self to write about. At least ideas that worked. But I said, "All right, I'll see what I can do."

Bruce A. looked back at his books. After a while he chose a few. "See ya tomorrow," he said, and went to check them out.

I watched him leave and caught myself grinning. But I felt nervous. I'd never done anything like this with a guy before. In fact, the only newspaper I ever wrote was the one I made only a single copy of and gave to Mom. I did it with rubber stamps and it took forever.

I thought about Bruce A. again. Maybe it would be okay to like him the whole summer. But what if he always had scabs? That would mean I'd always be sneering. Things sure could get complicated then.

Chapter Seven

Private Journal of Elyse Donaldson, World-class Writer.
Ideas so far: Rappelling, falling from great heights, scabs
Bruce A. Bruce A. Bruce A. Bruce A. Bruce A.

mulberry

I got up early the next morning, seven o'clock, to get ready for the newspaper job. I had a list of things to write about, which I'd spent so much time on I still hadn't had the chance to work on my book. I had folded and unfolded the list so many times that the paper was soft now and almost ready to tear on some of the creases. There were dirt smudges all over it.

I had written these ideas:
>Gossip Column
>Horoscopes
>Movie Reviews
>Book Reviews
>My Own Book?

At ten minutes after eleven I pulled up in front of Bruce A.'s house. I'd been riding around on my bike for about an hour and I would have been on time but I'd seen Patrick and Caleb and had taken the long way around the neighborhood so they wouldn't catch me. Luckily, I was far away from them or I might not have made it to Bruce A.'s place at all.

I knocked on the door that was painted a deep green. I could hear lots of noise and somebody young was crying. Somebody else was playing the piano. Maybe that was why the young person was crying. It was some awful piano playing. I stood outside for a while. On a hook near my head hung a flower pot full of tiny five-petaled flowers. They smelled good, and a fat bee buzzed in and out of them. There was a bike in the bushes next to the door and I noticed a crack in one of the windows.

After a bit I knocked again. Then I pounded. The door opened.

A boy about five or six years old stood in front of me. He was wearing a pair of too-big shorts. His feet were dirty. He looked like Bruce A. must have when he was younger. The little boy didn't say anything. An older girl pounded on a shiny black piano.

"Is Bruce A. home?" I asked.

The boy slammed the door in my face. "Bruce A.," I heard him laugh. "Bruce A. Bruce A." His hollering grew less and less loud.

I rolled my eyes and stood there for a minute more. I was turning to leave and go back home, hopefully not the long way, when the door swung open wide. It banged on the wall inside the house.

"See," the little boy said, "this girl's not as fat as the other one."

Bruce A. thumped the boy on the head with his knuckle.

The boy punched Bruce A. hard in the waist.

"Get outta here," Bruce A. growled at the little boy, who kept right on standing there like he hadn't heard a thing.

"I just wanna see if this girl's butt jiggles too," he said.

Bruce A. did not laugh. Instead he said, "Ignore Joshie at all possible costs. And come with me."

I followed Bruce A. into the living room. The older girl never looked up from the piano. Her blond hair hung in ringlets down her back and she bit her lip in concentration.

"Close the door, Joshie," Bruce A. said. The door slammed so hard I felt the air shake.

A beautiful woman came out of the kitchen. She held a baby on one hip.

"Mom," Bruce A. said. "This is Elyse Donaldson. She's going to be helping me with the newspaper."

"Are you a writer too, Elyse?" Mrs. A. asked. Her eyes were the same blue color as Bruce A.'s. Her voice was as soft as this lady was small. I couldn't believe that she had had ten babies. Maybe all those kids were a rumor.

I nodded my head. "Yes ma'am."

"She's pretty good," Bruce A. said. And then he started up the stairs. "We're going to my room."

"Nice to meet you, Elyse," Mrs. A. said.

"Nice to meet you, too," I tried to say back. But I'm not sure it came out that way. I was too surprised that Bruce A. thought I was a pretty good writer.

Bruce A.'s room was small. His computer sat on a long table made of a piece of countertop supported by file cabinets. Over the desk was a bulletin board that had newspaper clippings on it. Most of the clippings were about young people who had started successful businesses and were now making lots of money. The room was very neat. All the shelves were organized.

Anna-Leigh sat on the chair at the computer. I remembered Joshie saying that her butt had jiggled and I couldn't help but notice that it hung over on both sides of the chair. Suddenly I felt very sorry for her. She turned when Bruce and I came into the room.

"Hi, Elyse," she said. Her face was pink and I hoped she somehow hadn't known what I was thinking.

"Hey, Anna-Leigh," I said. I sat down on the twin bed made up with a purple-and-black Utah Jazz blanket.

Bruce A. was all business. As soon as I was settled he began talking about his plans for the one-page weekly newspaper. We shared our ideas for what we wanted to put in it. In the end I was put in charge of what Bruce A. called the fiction section. I would write and answer letters for a column called Dear Miss Know-it-all, I'd make up the horoscopes and, if I wanted, I could start my book and begin publishing it right there in the newspaper.

We decided the newspaper would come out on Sunday mornings, early, before Bruce A. went to church. As soon as they were passed out we would start layout for the next paper. All three of us had four streets to hand the papers out on. I made sure I didn't get Patrick and Caleb's street. I didn't want them chasing me around bright and early one morning each week. Let them chase Anna-Leigh. They were afraid of her.

Chapter Eight

Private Journal of Elyse Donaldson, World-class Writer.
Ideas so far: Cleaning house, going to the doctor, avoiding
two creeps   Why can't I think of anything to write?
I need an experience or two.

plum

Mom picked up Granny that night on her way home from work.

"Granny," I said, afraid for a moment that she might not remember me, afraid she might call me Addie again. Granny held her arms out and I ran over to hug her. Her blue eyes looked right into mine. Her slightly humped back pulled her over a bit, like she was leaning to tell me a secret. I felt like a giant near my grandmother. For a moment I felt like it was my job to protect her.

"Elyse," she said. Her neck smelled soapy. "You have a scratch mark right on your cheek. How did it get there?" Granny is always in charge when it comes to taking care of anyone. I touched my battle wound from the fight with Jordyn.

"I did it shaving, Granny," I said, and she slapped me on the bottom. Granny's white hair was thinning and I could see her pink scalp. I touched her soft hair with my hand and hugged her one more time. I was glad Granny was with us. Glad that she wasn't strange like she had been a few nights before.

"Is dinner done?" Mom asked Jordyn.

"Elyse still needs to set the table," Jordyn said.

"I'll help," said Granny.

"No, Mother," Mom said. "Elyse can do it alone. And anyway, this is your evening off. Nothing but rest for you while you're here."

"What do you think I do all day at that place you have me in, Sarah?" Granny asked. "Work in the steel mill? I have a maid come in whether I need it or not. I can go downstairs for each and every meal and eat with all those other ancient people. Oh yes, there is that strenuous game of bingo. But that's on Wednesdays." Granny came into the kitchen, where I was pulling out the dishes. She looked pretty in her pale purple skirt and embroidered blouse. Her white sweater had little flower buttons. I glanced down at my own T-shirt and shorts. I was glad I had changed before Mom and Granny got there. I didn't look too grubby, just a little wrinkled.

"I wish your mother wouldn't worry about me," Granny whispered in a rather loud voice; then she took the glasses and plates from me and started setting the table.

It was after dinner that Mom dropped the bomb on Granny. We were all in the living room sitting on our beat-up sofa and chairs, except for me. I was on Granny's lap, my feet pulled up so they wouldn't touch the floor, my nose nestled into her neck. I always climb up into Granny's lap, every Monday night when she visits us and every Thursday night when we visit her.

"You're probably breaking every bone in Granny's body," Jordyn said.

I ignored her and rested my head on Granny's shoulder. It felt so good to be held. Maybe there was a book idea about sitting in my granny's lap.

"Yes, Elyse," Mom said. "I don't think Granny needs you sitting on her." Jordyn squinched up her face at me in an I-told-you-so smile. "Go and mix up a box of brownies. I bought some last time I went shopping."

Granny's arms tightened around me. "Everyone needs a little love now and then, Sarah." I smirked back at Jordyn.

Mom was nervous, I could tell. Her eyes let me know she wanted me out of the way.

"You'll like these brownies, Granny," I said. "I make them so they're not too soft and not too hard.

They're just the right chewy." I got up and went into the kitchen. Since our living room and kitchen and dining room are practically one room I wouldn't have any trouble hearing, especially if I tiptoed around and kept one ear pointed at the door.

"Jordyn?" Mom asked.

"I'm going, Mom."

I could imagine Mom biting her nails. I peeked in at her. Yep, she was. The evening sun streamed in through our huge front window, setting Mom's light hair on fire, making her look younger than she is. Granny rocked, her back to me. The ceiling fan swirled, stirring up the warm air, the soft soap smell of Granny and the lingering odor of Hamburger Helper.

"Elyse?" Mom's voice was a warning, so I slipped back into the kitchen and got out the brownie mix. Then, trying not to make any noise at all, I listened to Mom and Granny.

"All right," Granny said. "They're gone. What is it this time?"

"Oh, Mother," Mom said. "Please. This isn't going to be easy for me."

Granny mumbled something under her breath, but I couldn't make out what it was. Neither could Mom.

"What was that?" she asked.

"I said, 'Here we go again.'"

I could imagine that Mom was sitting with her

hands covering her eyes but I didn't dare to peek in again.

"I've been worrying about you a little lately," Mom said.

Granny mumbled again.

"Don't do that, Mother. I hate it when you talk under your breath. You've done that all my life."

"I said, 'What's new?'" Granny said.

"And don't be sarcastic. It's mean."

Granny didn't mumble this time. "Let's not forget who's the First Mother." First Mother is something Granny always calls herself when she feels like Mom is trying to make her listen to or do something that she doesn't want to. It really bugs Mom.

"Mother. You are making a difficult situation even harder on me. Yes, as I normally do, I've been worrying about you. But this time I have good reason."

It was quiet in the living room and I leaned closer, trying to find out what was going on. I tiptoed next to the doorway, the box of brownie mix in one hand, and strained to hear. I was wondering if I shouldn't get a glass and hold it to the wall when Mom called in, "Elyse, are you making brownies?" It caught me off guard enough that I sucked spit down the wrong way and started to cough.

"No," I squeaked out. "I'm choking."

"Please do what I asked you." I could tell that Mom

59

was not too concerned with my choking to death right then, so I got a drink of water from the faucet, using my hand as a cup. I slurped fast so I could get back to listening.

"The brownies, Elyse," Mom said.

I tore the box open, trying not to make a sound. My stomach was in knots because of what Mom was getting ready to do.

"I've been worried about you being alone," Mom said.

"I've been alone for nearly a year now." Granny sounded agitated.

Mom cleared her throat. I took the plastic bag from the box and bit it open, then dumped the brownie mixture into a large plastic bowl. I got two eggs out of the fridge and cracked them as softly as possible. It took a bit of tapping because I didn't want to miss a thing from the living room.

"I know. It's been eight months since Daddy passed away. And I worried about you then, too. But remember? You refused to come home with us. You wanted to stay with your memories."

"I wanted to stay in my house over in Lindon," Granny said. "But *that* had already been sold."

My mouth was getting dry and my throat still felt choky, so I took a swig of milk from the jug before I poured a cup of it into the brownie mix. I added some oil, then stirred everything up with a fork. The orangy-yellow egg yolks broke open and for a moment reminded me of art class and a sunset I had painted.

"Let me get to the point, Mother," Mom said, rushing all her words together so she could get them out before Granny stopped her. "I want you to move in here with us. I haven't talked to the girls about it yet, but I know they would agree with me. Especially Elyse. She's been having such a hard time lately. I know she would truly enjoy you being here."

What? Mom thought I was having a hard time? What did she mean by that? Had Jordyn told her about the fight? Did she know I couldn't think up any writing ideas?

It was so quiet in the living room that I wondered if both Granny and Mom could hear the fork stirring against the plastic bowl.

"Sarah," Granny said. "I can't do that. I don't want to. I need my privacy and you need yours."

"I've got it all figured out, Mother. There's plenty of room for you here. You could help us. And we could help you."

"I won't hear of it. No."

With a stick of margarine I greased a pan; then I poured the batter into it and stuck it in the oven. I wanted to think more about what Mom had said about me having trouble, but I also wanted to know what was happening in the living room. I stood quiet, waiting. I could always think about me later.

I didn't have to sneak to listen in on the conversation now. Both Granny and Mom were loud.

"Mother, the incidents are becoming more frequent."

"What incidents, Sarah?"

"We've talked about them before. Don't you remember? You have been wandering around the building. You're losing things."

"The only thing I am losing," Granny said, "is my mind." She said it as a joke, I knew, but the silence that came into the room was thick and uncomfortable. Granny cleared her throat and said, "Lots of people lose things, especially at my age. That's not unusual."

My hands were cold and tears filled my eyes. Why did I feel so bad for Granny and Mom? The sadness plugged up my throat with a hard lump.

"But it's other things, too, Mother." Mom's voice was as sad sounding as I felt. "The nurse at the building called me at work a few days ago. She's worried about you too. You were out in the middle of the parking lot looking for Dad. You've gotten lost at Albertson's over and over again. You've been calling here in the middle of the night and you don't remember the next day. Sometimes you don't know me when I come to visit."

I hadn't known *all* this. Why hadn't Mom told me?

"Why haven't you ever talked to me?" Granny said. She sounded put out. "Why are you springing this on me all of a sudden?"

"I have talked to you." Mom's voice was soft and sad. "Over and over."

"You have *never* talked to me about these things. I would remember if you had. I have a wonderful memory." It sounded like Granny was getting ready to cry and it made my stomach tight to hear her voice sounding so afraid and alone and unsure of herself.

"Mother, you just don't remember. You can't remember. We've had talks about your forgetting and how serious I think this is. I'm afraid you're going to get hurt, or really lost. I want you here where I think you'll be safe. The girls are home for the summer."

Granny's voice got huffy. "I do not want to be baby-sat."

"I promise the girls won't coddle you. I want you to pull your weight. You'll not feel as useless here as you do over at the apartment building. Please consider it."

Granny was quiet. It took all my willpower to keep from peeking out at my mother and grandmother. I held tight to the countertop, squeezing until my knuckles turned white. The smell of cooking brownies drifted through the kitchen.

Why had I made such a point to listen in on this

private conversation? It only made all the good feelings of sitting on Granny's lap squish up into a hard little ball. I peered out the big kitchen window that looked over our backyard. The sky was turning purple with the coming night. The clouds were orange. A fat moon sat yellow and low over the mountains. Our two apple trees looked like dark monsters crouching against the fence in the twilight.

"John," Granny said. It scared me to hear her call for Granddaddy. "Johnny, I'm lost. Can you help me?"

"Mom, I'm here. I'm here for you." My mother's voice was soft and soothing. I went to the kitchen door. At the end of the hall I could see Jordyn. Had she been listening in on Mom and Granny too?

I stared at her a second, then looked in at Mom. She knelt at Granny's feet, both arms around her, talking in a whisper, saying things I couldn't hear. Suddenly I saw the four of us like a picture, one that I was seeing for the first time: Jordyn afraid, walking over to be near Mom; Granny confused and calling for her husband; Mom so sad that when she looked up at me I could tell by her eyes that she was hurting; and me watching all alone.

Chapter Nine

Private Journal of Elyse Donaldson, World-class Writer.
Ideas so far: Sitting in my granny's lap, making brownies,
worrying   What is going to happen to us all? And
why is Mom worried about me?

cerulean

Aunt Maggie, Mom's only sister, came the next evening. Granny was at her apartment. Aunt Maggie looks like Mom only she's taller and keeps her hair cut short. She's what Mom calls very fashionable, always wearing the latest styles. She drives a fancy car and is going to school full-time at the University of Utah so she can get her master's degree in nursing. She's a psychiatric nurse at one of the university's hospitals. She and Mom talked about Granny for a long time and worked out a schedule to help take care of their mother. Jordyn and I sat quiet in the living room and listened.

"I've switched my schedule around so I have weekends off," Aunt Maggie said. She wore a pretty denim dress that went almost to her ankles. Her freckled skin was the color of copper because of her tan. "I can come and get her early Saturday mornings. I wish I wasn't so busy with school and work, I could have her more of the time. Maybe I should postpone schooling for a while."

Mom looked a little worried. "You're almost done, Maggie," she said. "You've got to finish your degree. And things are going okay for me at work. Michael is letting me off every day at four. I think the girls will be fine." She glanced at Jordyn and me like she was weighing our abilities to take care of Granny in her mind.

"You know, she's always been around for us," Aunt Maggie said. "Remember when I had double pneumonia? She stayed at the hospital with me the whole time 'cause she knew I was afraid."

Mom nodded. "I hate to put her in an old folks' home. They always smell so funny." Mom wrinkled her nose at the memory of smells.

"Move her on the weekend and I can help," Aunt Maggie said. One of her dangly earrings caught the light from the lamp and twinkled. She pushed her gold-framed glasses up on her nose. "I bet I can get one of the guys at work to help us move her stuff. I think Jared has an old pickup."

"I'm kind of worried about Mother's things," Mom said. "I don't have room for everything here, but I hate

66

to get rid of it. I keep thinking maybe she's going to want some of it around. You know—later."

Aunt Maggie shook her head. "Sarah. I know you already know this, but Mother is not going to get better. Alzheimer's won't kill her. Unless she's in a car accident or something she's going to die of old age. So when we make this move, realize you can't keep everything from her past. There isn't room and she's not going to be using most of it. Eventually, she won't even remember any of it."

"I know," Mom said, nodding. "But I can't bear to get rid of it yet. I'm going to wait awhile and store it."

"I'll pay for the storage unit," Aunt Maggie said. "And I'll help with monthly expenses. Thank goodness Daddy left money for her. Care is so expensive."

Mom and Aunt Maggie looked at each other; then Mom got up and went over to her sister. They put their arms around each other and, like someone said go, they both started crying. Then they were laughing, then crying again.

I was embarrassed by the whole thing but sad, too. I tried to imagine Jordyn and me crying together about our own mom. I couldn't do it. Mom stayed young in my thoughts. And I was glad.

After their crying scene, Mom and Aunt Maggie went over to Granny's apartment. Sometime during the evening they convinced their mother to come to our house. She came that very night, way after midnight. I know because Jordyn and I stayed up, sitting in the dark living room, waiting. We didn't even talk, just sat quiet and waited.

The only light came from the streetlamp outside. It shone in the front room, bathing furniture and us with a pale light.

When the car pulled into the driveway, I was almost asleep.

"They're here," Jordyn said, and we both leaped to our feet and ran to the window. I was all the way awake now. I peered out at my mom and aunt and yes, my grandmother.

"Here goes nothing," Jordyn said. I looked at my sister but she had already turned from me and headed down the hall to her room. I couldn't tell if she was happy about Granny coming here. But I sure was. Happy, I mean.

The next morning Mom woke Jordyn and me early to talk about what she called "the new living arrangements." Granny was still asleep in my bed. I had slept with Mom.

"I don't mind if Granny lives with us," said Jordyn. Her hair was brushed and braided and she was dressed in shorts and a T-shirt. I could even smell her hair spray. How had she gotten ready so quickly? I was still rubbing sleep from my eyes. "But I refuse to share a room with *her*." Jordyn jabbed her finger at me. "She's too much of a slob."

I yawned big, opening my mouth wide in Jordyn's direction. "Oh please, Mother dearest," I said in a high, whiny voice. I clasped my hands together like I was praying. "I do want to share a room with my favorite sister. It would mean so very much to me. Perhaps I could curl up at the foot of her bed."

"You make me sick," Jordyn hissed at me. "And you look dumber than an old cow when you make that ridiculous face."

Mom gritted her teeth and said in a low voice, "There will be no more arguing. This is an extremely hard time in my life and I need to be able to depend on both of you. If you can't get along, fine. Don't talk to each other. But there will be no more fighting in this house."

Jordyn looked down at her lap and I yawned again, this time behind my hand.

"Now," Mom said. "I will not ask you to share a room. That would be hell for us all. But Granny needs a place of her own. At least for now. Her lapses are more frequent than they used to be, but she knows where she is enough that she would be uncomfortable having one of you stay with her." Mom looked at me.

69

"I was hoping, Elyse, that you wouldn't mind making the sacrifice. Will you give up your room for Granny?"

I hesitated for a second. It would be hard to leave my desk. That's the best thing I own. I got it at a garage sale for three dollars. I stripped and refinished it all by myself. "Sure, Mom. But the only place left to sleep is with you, and you snore."

Mom tried to smile. "I was thinking that you could have the sunroom."

I couldn't believe it. That room was big enough for me to squeeze my desk into, with a bit of furniture shifting. My summer luck was changing after all.

"Wait, Mom," Jordyn protested. "That's not fair. I want that room."

"Tough," I said. "Mom asked me, Missy Prissy. I get it." I made a face at Jordyn.

Jordyn looked past me like I wasn't there. "Can't we send Elyse to a retirement home? A fair trade, Granny for her. It'd be a lot easier."

Mom ignored both of us. I could tell it took all her strength not to yell. "I've given this a lot of thought," Mom said. Her voice was sharp. "Elyse's room is the closest to the bathroom. It's also in the front of the house, so it gets the morning sun. Granny needs a warm room. She's getting so thin that she's almost always cold."

Mom looked from me to Jordyn and I decided it would be best to keep my mouth shut. I didn't want to run the risk of losing my newfound luck. "And there's not as much to move as there would be with your room, Jordyn. No posters on the wall, not as many clothes or stuffed animals. And you need a closet. There's not one in that room."

"Does that mean you don't mind if I continue to use the floor as a large dresser drawer?" I asked. I grinned.

For the first time Mom seemed to relax. She smiled back at me. "Maggie and I spoke to Granny's doctor yesterday before we moved her here. He's aware of the situation. If there's any emergency, anything at all, you can call him."

I wondered what kind of emergency Mom meant but I didn't ask.

"My hours are changing at work. You know that. With Maggie helping with money I won't have to be gone so much." Mom leaned forward and took my hand and one of Jordyn's. I squeezed her hand tight and she smiled at me.

"It's not going to be easy, girls. Dr. Brackenbury warned me about that. Do you think we can do it if we work together?"

I nodded. From the corner of my eye I saw Jordyn nodding, too.

"And, Elyse, I've already made a cleaning deal with you. I won't forget it."

"Thanks, Mom," I said. I turned to grin at Jordyn but I never got the chance.

Granny wandered into the living room. She wore her nightgown, one spotted with pink flowers, but she had my old ski jacket on over it, and my snow boots.

"I'm lost," she said. We all stared at her. "This is the closest thing I could find to work boots. And they're too big." She raised the nightgown high with one hand and pointed to her feet, which were swallowed up in my black-and-gray snow boots. Her legs were very white and thin, her knees knobby. "How I can be expected to tromp around pulling weeds wearing something much too big is beyond me." For some reason I felt embarrassed. It made matters worse that my boots were too big for my grandmother.

Mom stood and walked over to Granny to help her.

"Let me help you put on something more comfortable," she said. They went back down the hall to my room.

I looked at Jordyn. Inside I was all cold with worry. Was she? I edged closer to my sister, trying to be careful. If I was really slow about it . . . there, my arm was pressed against hers. Jordyn looked at me. At first I thought she'd jerk away when I touched her, but she

72

didn't. I relaxed then, hoping the warmth of her arm would ease the coldness I felt inside.

"There's going to have to be a truce," Jordyn whispered. Her breath was minty smelling and clean.

"What?" I asked, even though I knew what she meant. Granny had confused me.

"We're gonna have to be friends, even if we do hate each other. You heard Mom say it herself: This is a hard time for her. We're gonna have to get along."

I looked at my sister. She was pretty, even this close. And I really did want to be her friend. Somehow, though, my mouth always got in the way. I was glad for this excuse to be on her side.

"All right," I said. "I agree to a truce." I reached my hand out to Jordyn. "Let's shake."

Jordyn took my hand and I heard Mom say, "Mother, these things are going to hurt your feet. At least let me put some slippers on you." They were still in my room.

Granny clumped into the front room. I felt all bug-eyed. Now she had on her clothes from the night before, but she was still wearing my snow boots.

Thwump, thwump, thwump. Granny marched around the table, gesturing at the dining room window with large sweeps of her tiny hands.

"Addie, it's storming to beat the band out there, and you want me to work in the garden with slippers on?

It's bad enough I'll be getting blisters from these old work shoes of Papa's."

"Mother?"

I looked at Mom when I heard her speak.

"Mother?" she said again. "Come back." I thought Mom would cry, but she didn't. She rushed over to Granny and took hold of her by both shoulders. "Come back. There is no rain. There is no garden."

"Why, Addie," Granny said, "you're ailing. I can see the rain clear." Granny pulled away and went and stood at the window. The sun, shining bright, streamed through. It splashed onto the table. "Well, it was raining earlier." Granny sounded like me when something doesn't go quite the way I think it should. Kind of afraid and stubborn at the same time. Granny clumped into the living room and sat in her rocker.

Mom turned then. Her face looked funny, like it was all stiff or something. "I have to get to work," she said to Jordyn and me. "She'll be fine, just keep an eye on her." Mom paused and asked, "Will you two be okay?"

We both nodded.

"Where's the Postum?" Granny called to us.

"Elyse, don't forget to get your things out of your room so Granny can move in."

After breakfast, without my even asking, Jordyn helped move my stuff. More than the truce, seeing Granny all confused made us allies, like we were fighting the common enemy. The one that had stolen our grandmother.

Chapter Ten

*Private Journal of Elyse Donaldson, World-class Writer.
Ideas so far: Forgetting when you're old, forgetting when
you're young, just plain forgetting   Granny's here.
She's acting weird.*

sepia

The sunroom is just as shabby as the rest of the
house, as far as furniture goes. There's an uncomfortable reading chair and a lumpy pullout sofa
bed. What makes this room so great are the windows.
There are six all together, two on each outside wall.
And there's even a ceiling fan with four lights pointing
down at the floor like big white flowers.

Granny clumped around the house, following
Jordyn and me as we carried armloads of books
and clothes and papers from my old room to my new
one.

"Where's Pa?" she asked again and again. We didn't
know what to answer. Should we say her father was
dead? It seemed mean to tell it straight out.

Sometime before lunch Granny came back to us, the

76

Granny I knew. She was walking down the hall when she suddenly stopped.

"What in the world am I doing in these ridiculous winter boots? It must be ninety degrees outside."

Jordyn and I were carrying my desk down the hall, each of us taking baby steps, trying to maneuver the bulky thing to my new room, where I could picture myself writing best-sellers while I looked out a window into our backyard.

"You wanted to wear them," I said. "Mom tried to get you to change this morning, but you . . ." I couldn't tell her the whole truth. "You didn't want to."

Granny looked at me as if I was crazy.

"Do you think I believe a story that ridiculous, Elyse?" she asked. "Why would you tell me such a thing?"

My mouth dropped open.

"I will talk to your mother," Granny said. "I can't believe you would make this up."

I felt my face start to turn red. Granny had never accused me of being dishonest before. I couldn't carry my end of the desk anymore. I set it down.

"It's true," Jordyn said. "What Elyse says is true, Granny."

Granny looked from me to Jordyn. Her bottom lip trembled. "It can't be," she said, almost like she was talking to herself. Granny stood there like she had lost her way or something.

"Let me help you," Jordyn said. She guided our grandmother toward the sofa. They shuffled together like all Granny's energy had melted away. I watched from my end of the desk.

It wasn't fair. I needed Granny to be okay. I needed her to hold me on her lap and laugh and not get weird. I needed her to be the way I remembered her before Granddaddy died, happy and fun and safe and trusting. Why was this happening? How could she accuse me of lying? My face grew warmer as I thought of Granny's words.

Jordyn knelt at Granny's feet. The boot slid off easily. Two bunched-up socks fell out and bounced onto the floor. One rolled under the sofa.

"No wonder these old things were hurting me," she said. "When I was a kid I did that very thing to keep my sister's too-big shoes on my feet."

Oh no, not Addie again.

Jordyn removed the other boot. Two more socks fell onto the floor.

"It was Addie's idea. The socks, I mean. Her feet were so much bigger . . ." Granny's voice trailed off. She sat on the sofa, her hands limp in her lap.

"I can't believe this is happening to me," she said.

"What?" Jordyn asked. "Don't worry about the

78

socks. I used to put wadded toilet paper in the toes of Mom's shoes and pretend her high heels fit me."

Granny's hands flickered in her lap.

"Not the socks," she said, and her voice sounded sad. "It's the here and there."

I don't know how, but I knew Granny meant her forgetting. It made a lump come up in my throat. But I couldn't go to my grandmother. Her words still hurt. Jordyn hugged Granny.

Jordyn and I worked hard moving my stuff. Later, when everything was in the new room, I started organizing things. I piled all my clothes into one corner where there were no shelves. I organized my books according to reading order. I pushed and shoved the furniture around the windowed room until there was enough space to squeeze my desk into place. I sat down in my straight-backed white chair and looked out over the yard. I could see Mount Timpanogos still wearing its crown of snow.

Jordyn made lunch, tuna sandwiches, and she and I ate in the living room with Granny, who rocked back and forth like she was out of energy. She ate too, but not like she enjoyed the food. It was more like she was doing us a favor—eating to make us happy.

Granny rocked until Mom came home, getting up only to go to the bathroom.

"Should I pull her chair to the table?" I asked Mom, when it was time for dinner. "Jordyn and I are pretty good at moving things now."

"No," Mom said, worry wrinkling her forehead. "I'll make her a plate." But Granny refused to eat. I didn't know which was worse: Granny crazy in her past or Granny not eating in her present.

Mom went to her own room to call the doctor. Jordyn carried a plate of cold food in to our grandmother. I followed and leaned in the doorway.

"Look," Jordyn said, holding the plate out in front of her. "I made dinner for you, Granny."

Granny rocked hard in the chair. She stuck her bottom lip out in a pout. She seemed so strange to me, almost like a little kid.

Jordyn leaned forward and with the fork moved around bits of lettuce and tomato.

"Elyse made the salad, Granny, see?"

"Poison." Granny said the word with such force that Jordyn jerked backward. I saw beans jump on the white Corelle plate. "Don't you think I know what is going on? It's a plot against me."

"What?" Jordyn asked.

I felt my body tense up like I was getting ready for a race.

Granny pointed from me to Jordyn, her gnarled hands making jabbing pokes at the air.

"I know what's going on. You can't fool me. I wasn't born yesterday, you know."

Jordyn nodded but her mouth had dropped open now and couldn't seem to stay shut, even though it opened and closed a few times.

"You're trying to kill me. I've seen it on *20/20*. People murdering their elderly family members."

Jordyn nodded again.

"I will not be duped," Granny said, and with her slippered foot she tried to kick Jordyn in the leg. Jordyn hopped back and then turned and walked to where I was. We both retreated to the table, even though we had finished our food long ago.

"Poison," Granny said again. "I will not be duped."

I looked wide-eyed at my sister. Her blue eyes were huge. I began to giggle.

"Don't laugh, Elyse," Jordyn said, but she grinned too. After a second we were both laughing.

"Poison." Granny's voice floated around the corner.

Jordyn and I wheezed anew. When was the last time I had laughed with my sister? It felt so good, like something was breaking open inside of me, pure and clean.

Mom came into the kitchen. "The doctor said depression is normal for Alzheimer's patients." She sat down at the table with us and I covered my mouth with my hand. I laughed through my nose, snorting.

"Poison," Granny crowed from the front room.

It felt like my guts were being laughed loose. Jordyn slapped at the table, making the forks jump.

"What?" Mom asked. But neither of us could tell her.

"So you're in on it, too, Sarah," Granny said from the doorway. She turned in a huff and left the room.

"What?" Mom asked again.

"Thank goodness she's still not wearing those snow boots," Jordyn said between laughs.

"That is not funny," Mom said. "Jordyn, Elyse. Stop that laughing right this instant. This is not a funny situation."

"Poison," I whispered, leaning toward my sister. I tapped at her warm hand and we laughed until I thought I'd never be able to stop. Mom smiled, her fingertips touching her mouth.

"Don't laugh at me."

I looked over at Granny. Her voice sounded as small as she looked. She stood in the middle of the kitchen, bent over a bit, her hands scrunched into fists.

"Mother," Mom said. She stood, and her chair scratched out an unhappy sound on the floor.

"Don't laugh at me. I'm doing the best I can. I can't help it. I don't want this to be happening. I can't help it that these things are happening."

Chapter Eleven

*Private Journal of Elyse Donaldson, World-class Writer.
Ideas so far: Poisoning relatives, new bedrooms, a script for
20/20   Can Dr. Brackenbury be right that it's safe
to have Granny home here with us?*

navy blue

The following Saturday Dr. Lauret came to help us move Granny's things from the retirement building. Dr. Lauret is the dentist Mom works for. He's a nice enough guy. When I was younger and would come and see Mom at work he'd let me dig through the prize box or take home a helium-filled balloon. Anyway, he'd brought his big shiny black four-door truck and he wouldn't let Mom pay for gas even.

"Come on, Michael," she said to him. We all stood in the driveway, Aunt Maggie, her friend Jared, Dr. Lauret and my family. The truck was parked in front of the house on the street, and Mom was waving a ten-dollar bill at the dentist.

He looked down at my mother and smiled at her.

His teeth were very white and also straight. I guess it wouldn't do to have a dentist who had crooked, yellow teeth. I mean, who could trust a guy who said he'd take care of your teeth if he looked like a squirrel? Dr. Lauret bent toward my mother and she didn't even move away from him. I noticed he was starting to go bald.

"I drove all the way from North Carolina to Utah when Kerry and I moved, and we paid for the gas together then. I can certainly pay for a little now," Mom said. "I already feel bad enough that you're not at the golf course."

Dr. Lauret looked around at the group of us. Aunt Maggie was grinning big. He winked at her. "You're right, Sarah. I'd never want to be called a male chauvinist." He took the money from Mom and, when she wasn't looking, handed it back to me. "Hide this," he whispered. I put the money in my pocket.

"Come on, Jordyn," Mom said. "You're riding with us. So are you, Mother."

Dr. Lauret went over to Granny and extended his arm toward her. "Your chariot, m'lady," he said. I rolled my eyes at how corny that sounded. But Granny, grumbling because she didn't want to move, took his arm and let him lead her to the cab of the truck. Dr. Lauret opened one of the four doors and helped her up the high step into the front. Then he motioned to Mom. "Should I help you in or not?" Mom looked at him a second, then grabbed his hand and got into the backseat. Jordyn got in too. Dr. Lauret ran around the truck and climbed in behind the steering wheel.

"Your mom's in love, Elyse," Aunt Maggie said as soon as the truck roared off around the corner. "And so's that doctor. Did you see the way he looked at her?" Aunt Maggie laughed. I followed her into the old Ford pickup that Jared would be driving. "They're both smitten. I can't believe your mother didn't tell me. And I'm her sister!" She laughed again.

"How can you tell she's in love?" I asked. The thought kind of bothered me.

Jared started the engine. It coughed, and blue smoke poured out of the back. Aunt Maggie ignored my question to look at Jared.

"Do you realize how environmentally unsound this piece of junk is?" she asked. He pretended not to hear and backed out of the driveway. His knuckles were white on the steering wheel. I wondered if they had had a fight during their drive from Murray. I hoped not. I liked Jared. He was always nice to me.

Aunt Maggie turned. I was glad I wasn't squished in between her and Jared because she had the same funny look on her face that Jared wore. I wondered for a second if Jordyn was sweating between two fighting adults or if Dr. Lauret was using the air conditioner in his truck.

"What did you say?" Aunt Maggie asked me.

"How do you know they're in love?"

Aunt Maggie smiled wide. She was chewing gum, Big Red, I think. I saw a flash of pink as she switched it from one side of her mouth to the other.

"Couldn't you tell, Elyse? The way they looked at each other. The way Dr. . . . I mean *Michael* leaned over toward her. And he must have touched Sarah four or five times, just while they were standing in the yard."

"Well, that's not good," I said.

"What?" Aunt Maggie asked. And her voice went up all high and funny at the end. "Why in the world do you say that? Don't you think your mom needs someone to live with? Someone to help make her happy?"

I was careful with my answer. "She has us," I said. "And if she meets someone else . . . well, then what about Dad?"

Aunt Maggie looked at me and her mouth dropped open. Now I was positive it was Big Red. The piece of gum sat on one of her molars. I couldn't help but wonder what Dr. Lauret would think of her teeth.

"Your dad's been gone a long time, Elyse," Aunt Maggie said.

I felt angry. "So?"

Jared followed the black truck, staying close to it so he wouldn't lose it in the traffic, I guessed. Not that you could really lose a truck as shiny as the one we were following.

"So, it's high time your mom moved on," she said. Just like that. She didn't even take a big breath.

"Don't tell her that," Jared said.

"This is none of your business," Aunt Maggie said to Jared, almost without moving her mouth. And then to me she said, "Life goes on."

"Yeah, but one dad is enough," I said.

Aunt Maggie wasn't listening to me. She wanted to argue with Jared.

"I really think your sister should be telling her daughter these things. Not you," Jared said. "I think you need to keep your mouth shut." He didn't look to the right or the left. But he did run a red light.

"Don't you ever tell me to shut up again," Aunt Maggie said. Her voice was low and dangerous.

"I didn't tell you to shut up," Jared said. "I said to keep your mouth shut."

"We still have a family," I said. "Especially with Granny moving in."

"You English majors are all the same," Aunt Maggie said. "Always arguing semantics."

Jared laughed, but it wasn't a funny laugh. "And you

psychology experts are always the same, thinking you can hold another person's feelings in the palm of your hand and wield them like a sword. Power trip. That's all it is to you."

Dr. Lauret had reached the place where Granny lived, a tall beige stucco building. Jared pulled up behind the truck. He gunned the motor a couple of times.

"Aunt Maggie," I said. "I think I have a right to not have extras in the family."

"There you go ruining the environment again," Aunt Maggie said. Her teeth were clenched.

Jared gunned the motor long and loud.

I got out of the truck and stood on the sidewalk, smelling exhaust. The sun beat down hot. The sky was almost cloudless.

Mom and Jordyn jumped out. They were both laughing. Mom was wiping tears from her eyes, even. Great, they had all the fun and I was with two people who were ready to kill each other.

And what about that Dr. Michael Lauret thing? I needed to get Mom alone for a while and find out if she really was in love with him.

But I never had the chance. Mom had already been to Granny's one weeknight with Aunt Maggie, and they had boxed everything and tagged it all to say whether it should go to storage or to our place.

Granny had tons of things stuffed into her two-bedroom apartment. The walls had been lined with years of pictures, decorated plates and things that Mom and Aunt Maggie had made in school. There were even things Jordyn and I had made in school. All Granny's closets had been jammed with clothes. Now boxes were piled ten high everywhere, and I didn't think we'd ever get it all moved. It took us a long time. I sure was glad there was an elevator in the building. I would have hated hiking up three floors.

We took the stuff Granny would be keeping with her to our house first. We broke down my old bed and put it in the U-Haul to go to storage. Then Mom and Dr. Lauret set up Granny's bed where mine had been before. They moved in a wooden rocking chair that was older than Granny herself, a hope chest and a long dresser with an ancient mirror. They let Granny decide which pictures she wanted on the walls.

Then we all headed over to the storage unit to finish the move. I could hardly walk. My arms felt like they were made of lead. One shoelace kept coming untied and I tripped over it so many times that I thought about going barefoot, but the asphalt was too dirty for that. It was at the storage place that Granny began sliding into the past. Maybe she was too tired or too frustrated or too hot, too, just like I was.

Dr. Lauret asked who was hungry and said he'd buy

for the whole moving crew if I'd decide where we wanted to eat. I could tell Mom was a little worried about taking Granny out when she was slipping through time, but she nodded for me to make a dinner choice.

We ate at Chuck-A-Rama, the all-you-can-eat place, for linner (a late lunch and early dinner combined).

"Go with Granny," Mom said to me, "and help her pick out something to eat."

"All right," I said. I got us each a plate and took Granny over to the salad bar.

"What do you want, Granny?"

She leaned real close to the bar and then stuck her pointer finger deep into the potato salad. "Some of that," she said.

"Granny, don't do that! It's really bad manners." I didn't know what else to say. Bad manners seemed a bit mild for someone sticking her finger into potato salad. Especially as far as Granny had stuck hers.

"Let me get my own food," Granny whined.

"How can I when you did that?" I pointed to the hole.

Granny smiled at me. "I'll not do it again. I wanted to see if it was hot."

"There's ice packed all around these things,

Granny," I said. "Nothing's hot here. It's all salad bar stuff."

"We shouldn't be in a bar," Granny said. Her voice was soft. "You know. 'Cause we're so young."

"*Salad* bar," I said, making the *salad* part come out louder. "Not a drinking bar. What else do you want?"

"This." Granny picked up a whole pickled beet. She took a big bite out of it. Then she spat onto the leafy greens that covered the ice. "That's the worst plum I've ever eaten in my life. I think it's poisoned me." She spat again before I had a chance to stop her. Some of the purple spit went into the carrot salad.

"Oh no," I said. My face turned red. "Granny. Let's go back to the table. I'll make your plate and bring it over to you. The way I would if you were a queen."

Granny licked the sleeve of her sweater. "Good idea," she said. "And I'll keep an eye out for spies. The ones that are poisoning the food."

I led her over to our table. "Keep her here," I said. "And whatever you do, don't get any carrot salad."

I went back to the salad bar and scooped all the purple I could out of the food. *If I had seen this on TV,* I thought, *I'd probably laugh my guts out.* But somehow cleaning up my grandmother's chewed-up beet wasn't very funny in real life.

I set the yucky food on an empty table and made a plate for Granny, avoiding beets. Then I got my own food and went to eat with my family.

A couple of guys dressed in jeans sat at the table next to us. They both had what Jordyn would have called funky hair: shaved high up on the sides, and what was left pulled back into ponytails. They wore earrings. One of them was eating carrot salad. I looked away.

"Addie," Granny said, jabbing me hard in the arm with her elbow. "Would you look at the facial hair on that girl over there?" She gestured with her potato-salad-poking finger at one of the guys at the next table. "She needs a shave."

"Shhh!" I said. But Jared had already heard. He was sitting across from us. He turned to look at who Granny was pointing at. Then he turned back.

"Granny," he said, "it's not nice to point, remember?"

"That's right," she said, and balled her hand into a fist. Now she pointed with that.

"She is the ugliest woman I have ever seen in my life," Granny said. Her voice wasn't that loud, really. But it seemed to slice through the air and cut everybody's conversations off. All the tables near our own wanted to see the ugliest woman Granny had ever seen in her life.

"And what on earth has she done to her head?"

Granny sounded surprised. "Shaved it? She should be shaving the hair from her upper lip and leaving that other to grow."

Jordyn looked at me, so embarrassed that the whites of her eyes looked red. Aunt Maggie was laughing behind a napkin. Jared got up for dessert. Dr. Lauret winked at the guys at the table, then started whispering to Granny, who answered all his questions in a very loud voice.

"Why yes, I see a dentist twice a year," she said. She sucked the partial bridge from her mouth and held it out in her hand. Tiny bubbles sat on the pink part that held the fake teeth, along with some bits of green beans. "But thith hath been hurting me."

I got up and went to the dessert bar. Here I'd been planning on eating all the sweets I could hold, and now my stomach was churning.

Jordyn came up to where I stood, near the bread pudding, and said, "Thank goodness she doesn't have a whole set of dentures."

I could only nod.

The last thing I heard from Granny in the Chuck-A-Rama was, "I have thum cornth on my feet, too. Can you look at thothe now, or would you rather wait?" Dr. Lauret said something about not working on corns, and after what seemed an eternity Mom signaled that it was time for us to leave.

I climbed into bed that night trying not to think of carrot salad. I pulled the sheet to my chin. It smelled a little like fabric softener. I lay on my back and watched the fan swirl in the semidarkness. My wide-open windows let in the cool air. The trees rustled and every once in a while the smell of roses blew in.

Big things were happening now, I thought. Not stuff like English grades or Patrick and Caleb bothering me again. It was serious this time. I could see Granny in my memory, sitting in Chuck-A-Rama with her bridge in the palm of her hand. I remembered her clomping along in my boots and crying because she was confused.

"I need someone to talk to," I said to the ceiling fan. But there was no one. The person I wanted to talk with was the one who had the problems I needed to talk about.

The fan spun slow circles and I shivered in my sweats. A breeze pushed the scent of roses through my windows again. I wondered if the smell came all the way from Mr. Clark's house.

In the purple night sky, one bright star twinkled at me. I crossed my fingers and wished on it. I felt a little dumb wishing on a star, but I needed all the luck I could get.

I squeezed my eyes tight.

"Granny, what are we going to do?" I said. "Oh, Granny."

There was a lump in my throat, one that needed to be cried out, but the tears wouldn't come.

So after watching the fan for a while, I turned on my side and finally went to sleep, without any answers.

Chapter Twelve

Private Journal of Elyse Donaldson, World-class Writer.
Ideas so far: Eating in restaurants with grannies who don't
know boys from girls or carrot salad from poison. People
can be weird, weird, weird.

jungle green

Granny's move took up a lot of time. It also took a while to get her settled in. She didn't like living with us much whether she was herself or not.

I did find time to write a crazy horoscope for our first paper, which came out the Sunday after we moved Granny to our place.

The Northwest Orem Gazette—this was Bruce A.'s title for the paper (I thought it was pretty dang boring, the title I mean)—was full of useful information for people in our neighborhood.

There was an interview with Scott, the old guy who owns a small grocery store on the corner in our neighborhood, about his business. There were my horoscopes and a letter (made up) to Dear Miss Know-it-all with an answer (also made up). I even wrote a book review

96

about *The Giver* by Lois Lowry. There was a schedule of articles we hoped to print in upcoming issues, a dot–to-dot (for kids) that we copied from Bruce A.'s computer, and a made-up weather forecast. All in all it was a good first edition. Especially the part about seeing what I had written in print. I decided right then and there I was going to make time or find time to start my own book. If I could come up with an idea.

The sun had barely peeked up over the horizon and already I was dressed. It was Sunday morning and I was ready to pass out papers so everybody in my whole neighborhood could have a chance at seeing what I had written.

I sat eating breakfast, thinking of what it would be like to be a famous and rich writer, when I heard someone knock on the door. It scared me and my cereal jumped from my spoon. Who could it be so early? Aunt Maggie had taken Granny after the move and wouldn't return her until late tonight. I looked out our front window. Bruce A.'s bike was parked in the driveway. I ran to open the door.

"Donaldson," he said, "I've come to walk with you while you pass out the papers."

"Oh." I couldn't think of anything else to say.

"Are you ready now?"

"I need to brush my teeth," I said. "Wait for me."

I closed the door and ran into the bathroom.

"Who's here, Elyse?" Mom asked from her room.

"Bruce A., Mom," I answered. I didn't bother to turn on the light. I just started scrubbing my teeth.

"What's he doing here so early in the morning?"

"He wants to pass out papers with me."

I swished water through my mouth and ran my fingers through my hair. Then I went back outside to Bruce A. He stood where I'd left him, holding a stack of printed pages. He smiled and I smiled back.

"You know what I like about you, Donaldson?" he asked. I shook my head and took my share of papers from him. We started down the sidewalk. The air was still cool and crisp feeling. There was a slight breeze blowing from Provo Canyon, clearing out the smog from Geneva Steel. We'd start today with clean air.

"The fact that you don't care what you look like."

"What do you mean by that?" I asked, feeling insulted.

"You have a glob of toothpaste spit on your face."

Oh no, I thought. "Where?" I asked.

He pointed to my cheek. I wiped at my face. He was right. Toothpaste spit. How had I missed that?

"And you never brush your hair," he continued.

"Yes I do," I said, even though that wasn't quite the truth.

"Well," said Bruce A. "You always have a kind of shaggy look. I like it."

I wasn't sure if the *shaggy look* was a compliment or not. But he had said that he liked it.

"Let's start with your section," Bruce A. said. We walked up the streets, each taking a side of the road and talking to each other across people's yards in the early morning. It was fun. We finished my four streets in no time at all. Then we headed toward Bruce A.'s section of the neighborhood. When all the papers were passed out, the sun had made its entrance and was a pure white-yellow color, too bright to even glance at. The breeze picked up and blew the newspapers we had taped to the doors, making them flutter.

"Want me to walk you home?" Bruce A. asked.

"Yeah, I guess so." I shrugged. Really, I did want Bruce A. to walk me home. But I didn't want him to know that. I mean, you just don't tell someone something like that: "Yes. I want you to walk me home. *Please,* please, walk me home." You kind of keep the begging part quiet and in your mind.

"Let's go the long way," Bruce A. said.

"Okay," I said.

"Can I hold your hand, Donaldson?"

I didn't know what to say, so I didn't say anything. I looked at the road because I was so embarrassed about his question.

Bruce A. grabbed at my hand and was only able to catch hold of my pinkie finger. For a second he held on to it and I thought that would be the most of our hand holding. Then his hand kind of crawled into the holding position.

We walked the long way home and Bruce A. talked about his family and what it was like to have nine sisters and brothers. My mouth talked to him about Granny living with us and what it was like to have her slowly leaving, and my mind raced, thinking about how nice his hand felt in mine. We reached my house too soon.

"I'll probably stop by on another day. If that's okay with you," Bruce A. said. He kind of looked past me when he talked, like maybe there was something really interesting on the roof.

"It's okay with me," I said.

I stood, quiet, on the small front porch, the sun breaking out over the mountains, sending fresh light out to me and everything around, and watched Bruce A. get on his bike. I felt glad Granny was gone. Just two days before, when Jordyn had come home from a date, Granny had slid open the living room window and pressed her face on the screen. "No kissing, Martha," she had shouted to Jordyn. Who knows who Martha is.

"See ya," Bruce A. said. And he was gone.

I sat outside awhile, thinking. Things, it seemed, were looking pretty good.

Chapter Thirteen

Private Journal of Elyse Donaldson, World-class Writer. Ideas so far: Holding hands with someone you like. This is a very private entry, so Jordyn and Mom, keep your snoopy noses out!! This means BOTH. OF YOU!!! I'm liking life right now. I like the writing for the paper. I like my stuff in print. I think I like Bruce A. Like Like Like Like. I like like, even.

sapphire

After the move, Dr. Lauret and Mom started going out together every Saturday night. Here I'd been enjoying Saturdays because I spent them working on the newspaper. And because Bruce A. and I were getting to be better friends. And because we didn't have to worry about Granny over the weekend. And then what happens? Mom starts dating a complete stranger.

Okay, Dr. Lauret isn't a complete *complete* stranger. Mom has been working at his office since I turned nine. And I do see him twice a year for my regular checkups. And he does share an office with my orthodontist, so I see him each time I go in to have my braces tightened or to fix a loose wire or something. But that is practically a complete stranger.

Each Saturday morning I'd wake up and think, *All*

right! I'm going to Bruce A.'s house to work on The Northwest Orem Gazette. *We're going to work with Anna-Leigh and he might sit close to me.* Since our hand-holding experience that one morning, seeing him with his hair all messed up didn't bother me like it would have if he had been another guy.

And now Mom had to go and do this. I wondered if it was some kind of plan.

"Let's see if we can make Elyse miserable on Saturdays," I imagined Dr. Lauret saying to Mom over the open mouth of a patient.

"How?" Mom would ask. The patient, preferably Caleb or Patrick, would roll his eyes from side to side, listening to the conversation.

"Let's start dating!"

Then Mom and Dr. Lauret would laugh over my soon-to-be-ruined Saturdays. To cheer myself up after imagining something like this, I'd have Dr. Lauret hit a nerve in Patrick's or Caleb's tooth.

To make matters worse, these two old people were seeing each other because they *liked* each other. The same reason I worked on the paper, because I liked Bruce A. And maybe they liked each other better than I liked Bruce A. They *had* been kissing one night. I witnessed it with my very own eyes. A long kiss. Had they both brushed before it happened, the dental assistant and the dentist?

I had a couple of questions about this kissing stuff. First, why did they have to do it right in public on our front porch? In front of the whole neighborhood, including Nosy Nikki. Second, why did they have to do it at all? I finally flashed the front porch light off and on a few times, like I'd seen in an old movie, to break things up.

Was this love, like Aunt Maggie said? What in the world, or maybe I should say what in heaven, could my dad be thinking about all this? I mean, if he thought anything at all. Maybe angels don't think. Maybe Dad's not an angel.

Things were getting too complicated for me. I wanted everything to stay the way it had been. With everybody not sick and everybody out of love. It only seemed fair. Then I could go about my business without worrying about what was happening to who.

So on the third Saturday morning after Granny moved in, I woke up all mad about what I knew would be happening that night between my mom and her tooth doctor. I grouched over to Bruce A.'s house. Joshie let me in.

"The fat girl is already here," he said. He was eating a large ice-cream cone.

"Don't say things like that," Mrs. A. said to Joshie, and then she offered me an ice-cream cone too.

"No thanks," I said. "I already had breakfast."

"Well, so has Joshie, but he really wanted one and it does have some good ingredients in it."

I smiled a forced, weak smile and climbed the stairs to Bruce A.'s room.

The door was just barely open, so I walked on in. Anna-Leigh was pressed up against Bruce A. Kissing him. I couldn't see anything of Bruce A. except his eyes, which were looking at me while she kissed his face!

I felt a stab in my stomach, which I was sure was the way a knife would feel. My eyes felt like they had popped in and out of my head a few hundred times. My face burned with color.

"Well," I said, not knowing quite what to do. All this kissing. First Mom and Dr. Lauret and now Anna-Leigh and Bruce A. What was my world coming to?

Anna-Leigh turned to look at me. "Oh, Elyse," she said. "I didn't hear you come in." Her face pinkened.

"It was those sucking noises you were making," I said, even though I really hadn't heard anything except the blood pounding in my ears.

Bruce A.'s face turned dark red through his tan.

Too much blushing going on for me, I thought, but I said, "I don't think you'll be needing my services anymore," and threw my notebook of horoscopes and Dear Miss Know-it-all questions and answers on the bed. "I quit."

104

"Wait," said Bruce A., moving around Anna-Leigh. "It's not what you think."

"Good," I said.

"We—we're doing an article on kissing . . . ," Bruce A. said, stammering.

Anna-Leigh nodded.

My eyes squinched up.

"Well, thanks for involving me," I said, and left.

"Going so soon?" Mrs. A. asked, still making ice-cream cones as I ran past her and out the door.

I didn't have time to answer. All I could do was run, as fast as possible, for home. *How could he?* I kept thinking. There were tears sitting in my eyes, wanting to splash down my face, but I willed them to stay put until I was in the privacy of my own room.

Jordyn was in the living room with Carli, a friend from school. "That didn't take long," she said when I came panting into the house.

"Thanks a lot!" I shouted at her, and started to bawl. Right there in front of Carli.

"Elyse?" Mom walked into the living room from the kitchen, where she was working on dinners to freeze for the next week.

"I'm busy!" I shouted at her. "Everyone just leave me alone. I mean it! I don't want to see anyone. Not even the President of the United States." Then I slammed the door to the sunroom. I threw myself on the sofa bed and sobbed into my pillow. I cried for a long time. And no one came to check on me, either.

After a while, I lay on my back and thought of the few weeks the three of us, Anna-Leigh, Bruce A. and I, had worked together. A pain came into my throat when I thought about us laughing. It was almost like someone had died. No, that was wrong. I rolled over onto my back and looked at the ceiling fan. It was like some*thing* had died.

"Our friendship is gone," I said, my voice a half whisper, half groan. Things felt very painful to me. It even seemed to hurt when I breathed, but that might have been because I had run so far.

I sat up at long last, determined to write my sorrows down for posterity, whatever that meant. In fact, now, at last, I'd have time to work on my novel. No more Miss Know-it-all for me.

I was mad all day. So mad I even cleaned up the bathroom without being asked. Then I cut the grass. Mom kept watching me from the window. Once I caught her and Jordyn *and* Carli watching me, but they hid when I stopped and glared at them.

At five-thirty Mom started to get ready to leave on her date.

That made me all the madder. Didn't she know how I felt? Sure, I hadn't talked to her, but still, wasn't it obvious the true pain I was in? What Mom was doing to me by going on this date was like ripping a Band-Aid off a sore that had a lot of hair growing around it. My heart felt pained. And a little lonely. Already I missed Bruce A. and Anna-Leigh.

I stomped around the house awhile, trying to communicate to Mom exactly how I felt. She wasn't bothering me any. In fact, she was leaving me alone just like I had asked her to. What a terrible, grouchy day this had become. I hated it.

I was so angry that I finally decided to talk to Mom, even though I wasn't sure what I was going to say. Definitely, though, I was going to give her a serious talking-to.

"Mom?" I pounded on the bathroom door. I could hear water running down the sink. She was probably wasting Utah's Precious Resource. That phrase was from an article Bruce A. had done on recycling here in Utah. I felt a ping in my heart, remembering *The Northwest Orem Gazette*.

Mom came to the door, brushing her teeth. Of course. She'd have to have clean teeth to go out with a dentist.

"Mom," I said again, only louder this time. Mom kept standing there, brushing her teeth, her purple toothbrush making small circular motions.

"What, Elyse?" Mom spoke through the foam.

"Where are you going?"

"Out."

Grrr. It was obvious Mom was enjoying brushing her teeth and bugging me at the same time.

"I know that," I said. "I mean, where?" My voice sounded as angry as I felt. But I couldn't change it. I didn't want to.

Mom ignored my tone; she just raised her eyebrows, then answered me. "Not that I need to give you any information, but Michael and I are going to the Ruby River." Mom went in and spit into the sink. The water came on in the bathroom again.

"So why aren't you dressed up?" I asked. "It's an expensive place, isn't it?"

"Well, kind of, yes. You can wear jeans," Mom said. "It's like a country-and-western restaurant."

"Gross," I said. "Country and western. Well, I don't think you should go anyplace like that."

"And why not? I've got to put on my makeup. Come talk to me in here."

"No," I said. But I went into the bathroom anyway and sat on the toilet. "You've got on enough makeup already."

"I washed it all off when I showered," Mom said. "See?" She leaned close to me. So close our noses touched and she was all blurry. I was too angry to play.

"Quit it," I said. "You're going to ruin my eyes."

108

Mom pulled away and looked at herself in the mirror.

"I think you should stop seeing Dr. Lauret," I said.
"The only thing it's good for is your teeth."

Mom gave me The Look. "Oh you do, do you?"
she said. Her hands were on her hips, the mascara
brush pointing at me. "And why is that?"

"Because he's old, Mom."

"Elyse, he's only two years older than me."

"Well, he's divorced."

Mom laughed. "So?" she said, and faced herself in
the mirror again.

"So, your husband is just dead. Being divorced is
worse."

Mom was brushing mascara on her lashes, opening
her mouth in a long O to get at the bottom ones. She
stopped again and turned to face me. She looked at me
a moment, then turned to the mirror again.

I kept on talking. "Death and divorce both prove
something. Those two *d*'s are proof of stuff," I said.

"And what's that?" Mom asked.

"That neither one of you can stay married. So why
try again?"

Mom looked at me, then reached for her lipstick.
She began lining her lips with a soft berry color.
"That's not a very nice thing to say, Elyse," she said
when she finished. "First of all, I didn't want your dad

109

to die. And I'd probably still be married to him if he hadn't. Second, I'm dating Michael. Dating him. Not marrying him. And third, should I tell you that I don't want you seeing Bruce A.?" Mom pointed at me with the lipstick.

Uh-oh, I thought. *I'm on bad ground.* I swallowed.

"No," I said. "My seeing Bruce A. is different. Very, very, very different."

"And how is that?"

"We see each other only in the professional newspaper sense. At least, we did." A lump came up in my throat. I tried to swallow around it but I couldn't, so instead I coughed.

"What happened today?" Mom asked.

"Nothing." A huge part of me wanted to tell Mom everything, but I couldn't. It was too embarrassing.

Mother leaned close to me again. "Then why did I see you holding his hand the other morning? Was it for the gossip column?"

My face went red. "Maybe it was, maybe it wasn't," I said. "That's finished anyway. At least I wasn't kissing Bruce A. in front of the whole neighborhood. At least I wasn't doing it right in front of Nosy Nikki."

"*I* am not twelve years old. *I* have had two babies of my own. *I* am allowed to kiss men. *And* hold their hands." Mom sounded angry.

"The only man you should be kissing," I said, "is

110

Dad. You know that. And Dr. Lauret should be kissing his wife."

"Oh, Elyse," Mom said.

Mom's voice was so sad sounding that I suddenly felt sorry for myself.

"We need to talk," she said.

The doorbell rang.

"Mom," Jordyn called. "Dr. Lauret is here."

"Ask him to wait for me a few minutes. Something important just came up," Mom called back, and she shut the bathroom door. Then she turned and looked at me. Her eyes were pretty.

"Your dad and I were great friends. I loved him very much. I still miss him," Mom said. "Death is not something that can be fixed."

"I know that, but don't you see?" I asked.

"Yes, I see. Now I want *you* to see. I can't stay lonely any longer. I don't want to."

"But, Mom, he's divorced." I'd never really thought of Mom being lonely before. I mean, she had me and Jordyn. And now Granny.

"That's okay with me," Mom said. "Michael is a nice guy. I like being with him. I'm happy."

"What about Granny," I said. It wasn't a question, it was a reminder. "She loves you."

Mom hugged me up close to her. "I've got to go," she said. "Michael's waiting."

"Guess Granny isn't what you had in mind, huh?" I said.

Mom grinned. "Not quite."

Mom walked out of the bathroom and I sat down on the edge of the tub. The room smelled like my mother, all soft and warm, kind of perfumy.

I dropped my head in my hands. Dad wasn't coming back, I knew that. And although I missed him, it was more the idea of having a dad that I missed. I'd known that all along.

I stood up and looked at myself in the mirror. I made faces at myself. I stuck out my tongue. I checked my teeth. Yuck. I guess I would just have to get used to Dr. Lauret. But I didn't really feel like getting used to him. Who would even want to date Dr. Open-your-mouth-and-say-Aaaah?

I started thinking about Bruce A. How dare he hold my hand and kiss Anna-Leigh? How had I allowed myself to get caught in the middle of a love triangle? This could be on television. I heard an announcer's voice in my head: "Stay tuned and listen to this year's greatest talk show hosts find out about . . . Love Triangles and the Twelve-year-old." I wondered if they could pay me enough to wrestle it out with Anna-Leigh on TV. I decided no. Since she could beat up Patrick and Caleb, I wouldn't stand a chance.

I got into the bathtub and lay down. I could feel the

112

drops of water from Mom's shower soaking into my clothes. I folded my hands on my chest and started thinking about other stuff. Like, how would it be to have your husband die, then have your father die, and finally have your own mom acting wacky?

That was a better story for television. Or wait a minute! This could be for my novel. I closed my eyes and wrote an imaginary letter to Geraldo, suggesting that he and Phil and Sally, and any other talk show host, retired or not, should all get together and interview me for a two-hour spot on feeling confused at age twelve.

Chapter Fourteen

*Private Journal of Elyse Donaldson, World-class Writer.
Ideas so far: At age twelve I am trapped in the middle of a
steamy and sordid love triangle (look up definition of sordid).*   *Things aren't going so well. I think my heart
and throat are cracking in two.*

jasper

"This is Granny's medicine," Mom said. She stood in the kitchen at the sink with the small bottle of pills in her hand. Jordyn and I sat at the table. Granny was still asleep. Mom would be leaving soon for work. Every morning for the past two weeks she had been giving Jordyn and me this same speech. I practically had it memorized. "She gets one pill before breakfast and one at night before bed. *I* will be giving these to her. You don't have to worry about this at all."

"So why are you telling us, then?" I asked. "Why again? I can tell you what you're going to say next."

"Granny has been trying to take her medicine more than once a day. I want you to know, no matter what she might say to you two, that I have already given it to her. Don't *you*."

"You've told us already," Jordyn said.

Mom kept talking. "The doctor said it'll make her dizzy. The last thing I need is her falling down. I'm going to keep the bottle up here over the fridge. But remember, no matter how much wheedling she does, Granny has already had what she needs for the day. I'll see to it."

"You tell us this every day, Mom," I said.

She ignored me. "Yesterday I found a tuna sandwich with one bite taken from it stuffed between the sofa cushions. There were also some peach halves and a clump of cottage cheese there."

"I didn't do it," I said.

"Me either," Jordyn said.

"I didn't think you did. But you two have to watch Granny. She must eat or she'll get sick."

"The last time I watched her," Jordyn said, "she blew her nose in the bread. And stuffed it into her pocket like it was a hanky or something."

"It was gross," I said.

"That's not going to change," Mom said. "It's your responsibility to see that she has a snack and lunch. I'll help her with breakfast and dinner."

"That's no big deal," I said. I had been worried that

maybe we would have to make sure Granny made it to the bathroom all the time or something.

"Are you taking turns working with her?"

Jordyn nodded. "We trade off days. And lots of times Laurel or Brooke or Carli comes over. They help me out."

Mom smiled. She looked pretty, even though I could tell she was tired.

"I keep telling you these things because I love Mother. And I love you two. I want things to go well. That's why you get the lecture each morning."

"I think we've got it good now," I said. "I'm pretty sure I could say the speech for you anytime you needed."

"I'll remember that, Elyse."

"Mom, what do we do when Granny . . . changes while she's eating?" asked Jordyn.

"I don't know," Mom said. "She'll argue with you if you try and tell her something isn't the way she thinks it should be. I've talked to Dr. Brackenbury about her changing. There's nothing really we can do to stop it. I guess, if it's not dangerous, you should let her believe what she thinks. We can't keep what's happening from happening. Let's just love her and be kind."

Mom started part two of the lecture, telling us the different things to do with Granny each day: exercise

116

(we decided walking was best), making sure if she got dirty that we helped her change her clothes, seeing that she ate, but not too much.

"Listen, Mom," Jordyn said. She reached out and touched Mom on the shoulder. "We love Granny too. We know what we're supposed to do. You don't have to check up on us anymore."

"I'll still call you every day at lunchtime to check on the three of you. And there's that Alzheimer's Hotline number. It's by the phone."

"We know, Mom," Jordyn and I said almost at the same time.

"And you know you can call me at work."

"Yes, we know."

"And if there's a problem, not an emergency, but a problem, Nosy Nikki across the street said you could call her."

Nosy Nikki has been in the neighborhood before the streets even went in, I think. She's old and wrinkled and wears a different-colored wig every day and all kinds of animal-skin–type clothes. Zebra pants, leopard dresses, tiger shirts. They're always skintight. She also has really long fake fingernails that she does herself. She lives right across the street from us in a house that looks just like ours. We've called her Nosy Nikki almost since the day we got our telephone connected. That's when she started calling us to let us know she could see us talking to her on the phone. I'm not kidding.

Anyway, she's always looking out her windows to see what's going on. She's nice enough, but you can be sure that she knows all your secrets. At least that's what I overheard Mom tell Aunt Maggie.

"Yuck," said Jordyn. "I hate having her involved. I always feel like I'm being watched when I'm anywhere near her house. Including in my own bedroom . . . if my curtains aren't closed."

"You feel like you're being watched because you *are* being watched," I said.

"I'm sure I've made this worse," said Mom. She squished her eyes shut and made a face like she had made a big mistake. "I've asked Nosy Nikki to check in on you two every once in a while."

"You *have* made it worse," I said, groaning. "We're doing fine."

"Oooh, Mom." Jordyn sounded like someone had punched her in the gut. She dropped her head into her hands.

"To be safe," Mom said. "Think how happy you're making a lonely old woman." Mom grinned at us and finished getting ready to leave.

She had barely pulled out of the driveway for work when the telephone rang.

"Hello, Nikki," I heard Jordyn say. "Yes, I can see

you through the window. No, you don't need to get your poodle to wave at me, I can see him looking over here too."

One of these days, I thought, *I'm gonna close the blinds right when she's looking through the window and talking to us on her phone.*

Mom was right about Granny being a pain in the neck to feed. Some afternoons, when she felt fine, she ate small portions of what Mom would think was a perfectly balanced meal. Other days, when she wasn't quite right in her mind, she ate like there was no tomorrow. She even tried to hide food away in her room. I found a stash of really stinky stuff in the corner of her closet. There were times when Granny felt depressed and she didn't want anything to eat. She wouldn't even drink her Postum.

Some mornings Mom's coaxing would wake me up.

"Mother, you need to eat this," I'd hear Mom say. And Granny would grunt an answer and Mom would start bribing. "An extra-long walk today with Elyse, Mother. Just eat a few bites. I want you to be strong."

"I don't want to be strong. I want to be dead," Granny would answer.

"Mother, you may as well know it now. You're going to outlive the world, so you better eat. You'll get sick if you don't eat."

"I want to be sick," Granny said. "I want to die."

"Mother, please don't say that. I want you to be as healthy as you can be."

One morning I heard Granny say, "Sarah, I love you. Oh, I love you. You and Maggie and the girls have tried so hard with me. But can't you just let me go?"

Mom's voice got loud. She wasn't yelling and I probably wouldn't have heard so well if I hadn't been in the room right next to the kitchen.

"No, Mother, I will not let you go. I love you too, and I will keep you healthy as long as possible."

"But my life is slipping past like sand through an hourglass." Granny had taken to watching a lot of TV in the daytime. She was always quoting *Days of Our Lives*. That's a soap opera.

Mom chuckled.

"I'm serious," Granny said. "Everything is so strange now. Sometimes I find myself in places I shouldn't be. It's a confusing world."

"One bite, Mother."

I came into the kitchen, still dressed in my pajama sweats. One good thing about sleeping in something like this is that I am always dressed if necessary.

Mom held a spoonful of eggs out to Granny. They wobbled a bit. Standing in the doorway, I felt a burst of love and sadness for my mom and grandmother.

I ran over and squeezed them together in a hug.

"You both are so great," I said.

Granny took a deep breath. "What would Ivan McCloud think of me?" she asked. Ivan McCloud is the anchorman on *The Sun Is Up* morning show, which comes out of Salt Lake City. "I'll eat," she said.

"And I'll change clothes so we can take an extralong walk," I said.

"After *you* eat," Granny said.

"Right. After I eat," I said.

Chapter Fifteen

Private Journal of Elyse Donaldson, World-class Writer. Ideas so far: Being lonely when you're as old as Granny or Nosy Nikki, being lonely when you're as old as Mom, being lonely when you're only twelve   I love having Granny around, even if she's different sometimes.

goldenrod

On my free days, the days I didn't have to stick so close to home and help out with Granny, I sometimes rode my bike, enjoying the sun hot on my skin and the thought of no school. I'd go to the library and stand in front of the D section of fiction books for young adult readers and imagine eight titles with my name on them. Sometimes I'd just lie outside in the grass, looking at the stained-glass window that covers an entire wall of the library, and think of book ideas. But mostly on my days off I was lonely.

I missed working on the newspaper and I missed seeing Bruce A. I thought about him a lot. It had been fun working with Anna-Leigh and Bruce A. It had even been fun seeing Joshie and wondering what weird thing he might say when I got to the door. I felt sadder still when I found copies of *The Northwest Orem Gazette* taped to my door. They were working without me.

"This is an idea for a book," I said one morning after breakfast, and sat down at my desk. I could hear Granny and Jordyn moving around in another part of the house.

But I was too sad to write. How long had it been since I had seen Bruce A.? Two whole weeks? Why was I still missing him? How come it wasn't getting any easier? Why didn't he insist that I talk to him on the phone when he called for me? I had refused three times because I was still feeling . . . I don't know . . . let down.

How could he hold my hand and then kiss Anna-Leigh? I wondered.

It's not what you think sounded in my brain again and again. I saw Bruce A.'s blue eyes, surprised at being caught. I wondered what my own face had looked like. Had my eyes bulged? Had my mouth dropped open? Could Anna-Leigh and Bruce A. both tell I was shocked?

I looked into my mirror and tried to make my eyes bulge. I couldn't do it. But I was able to get a pretty good I-don't-care-at-all look. I crossed my fingers, hoping that that was what I had looked like, even though I was pretty sure it wasn't.

Granny came to the door.

"Feel like going on a walk with me?" she asked.

"Yeah," I said. "Let me change my clothes first."

On the mornings Granny was herself, she and I walked before it got too hot. By noon the air was always on fire, so we'd have to go early. The snow on Timpanogos was melting fast. This summer was a burning one.

"Let's go see Mr. Clark's garden, Granny," I said when I came out in shorts and a plain white T-shirt that I had thought I might sometime decorate my own self. We visited Mr. Clark every walk. "He might be weeding and then we could help."

"Of course I'll help, Elyse," Granny said. She had on a pair of light blue polyester pants and a thin flowered cotton shirt. I grabbed some extra breakfast and was still chewing it when Granny started out the door. I didn't even have a chance to see if there was any French toast stuck in my braces.

What the heck, I thought. *I'll suck them clean once I get to where we're going.* I hurried after Granny.

Mr. Clark is one of the neighbors who has always visited us. He comes to our door with huge bags of vegetables picked straight from his garden. He told Mom how to fry the summer squash in butter and even sent over a recipe for fried green tomatoes, which he said his wife used to make all the time.

I always visit Mr. Clark too. When Granddaddy died, Mr. Clark helped me not to feel so sad. We play cards together, or checkers. He's even taught me how to play chess. I'm not that good, but I have fun playing the game with Mr. Clark. He's my friend.

Granny and I walked the long way to Mr. Clark's house, going around the block, passing a church and a small park. A pregnant lady with two young children sat in the shade of a tall pine tree there.

"You're a lot like Addie was, Elyse," Granny said. She held my hand and her skin felt thin and cool. "I always envied her because she was so tall and slender, as you are."

"I hate looking like this," I said. "I hate being taller than most of the kids in my classes. Including the boys."

In the ditch beside us, water flowed fast. It came from the mountains and was cold enough, I knew, to make my legs ache. I wondered where the unused water went. Did it circle into the sky, following the giant arrows my science teacher used to show evaporation? Or did it run on and on until it made its way to an aquifer?

"Well, Addie hated being tall too. And that was in the days when hardly anyone was big." Granny smiled. The sun lit up her head, making her hair look pure white and her scalp very pink. "Pa would tease her, even though he was tall himself, and ask 'How's the weather up there?' "

"I'm glad no one says that to me," I said.

"Oh, it bothered Addie, all right."

When we turned onto the road that ran near the school I looked everywhere for Patrick and Caleb. I could only see one kid, on Rollerblades. I breathed a sigh of relief. That was another thing about leaving the house early: I missed those two. It was a pain trying to schedule my whole outdoor existence around them, but I did it to keep safe.

Granny kept smiling over her memories of Addie.

The blader came closer. It was Bruce A. I could tell it was him even before he got close enough for me to know for sure.

"Hurry, Granny," I said. But she was talking to a tiny white poodle that had red ribbons tied to its ears. I started sucking hard on my braces.

Bruce A. slid up to where we were and sent a spray of rocks and dirt into the air. The wheels on his blades made a tiny *screech*.

"Donaldson," he said.

I looked at him with my practiced I–don't–care–at-all look.

"Oh, Bruce A.," I said, like I was surprised. My heart beat hard.

He had been skating around for a while, I could tell, because his face looked hot and it was a little pink.

"Listen," he said, adjusting his black-and-blue wrist

guards like he was nervous or something. And then he didn't say anything at all. He stood there looking first at me, then at the sky, then at me again.

Granny finished talking to the dog. She came up beside me and stood there.

"Hello, Mrs. Ivie," Bruce A. said.

"Hello," Granny said. "Do you two need a little moment together? We're almost to Alfred's house. You can talk there."

Bruce A. nodded and I shook my head.

"Well, let's walk on up to the corner and then I can sit on Alfred's stoop while you chat."

We all started up the street. The only sounds were the wind that blew hot puffs of air through the trees every once in a while and the wheels of Bruce A.'s Rollerblades.

Two-timing newspaper writer, I thought.

Mr. Clark was working in his garden when the three of us reached his house.

His garden is great. It takes up nearly all his backyard. From where I stood, I could see the slender stalks of plants pushing through the dark brown earth. Some were being trained up wooden sticks. The vines of squash and watermelon trailed in one corner, climbing toward the porch.

"Hello, Mr. Clark," I called.

He stood, straightening his back like he was stretching himself out. He gazed over the small sea of green to where Granny, Bruce A. and I stood, outside his fence.

"Hello, Elyse," he said, waving to us. "Come on in and visit. And bring that beautiful grandmother in with you."

Granny looked at me and her cheeks pinkened. "Nonsense," she said. But she kept on smiling and walked through the chain-link gate.

I started to follow but Bruce A. said, "Elyse," so I stopped. He had never called me Elyse before. It sounded kind of nice when he said it. Pretty, even.

Wait, I thought. *He's a two-timer. He was creepy to me.*

"Talk to me," he said.

"What do you want me to say?" I asked.

"Well, nothing, I guess. I want you to listen to what I have to say."

I leaned against the fence and looked at Bruce A. He sure was cute. I tried not to notice that and just gazed at him with my I-don't-care-at-all look, but the cute part kept getting in the way. *Two-timer,* I thought, to help myself not see the cuteness. *Creepy creep.*

"I need you on the paper."

I looked at him some more.

"I need you to work on the articles. The stuff you write is funny. You're funny. It's been harder doing

128

it without you." Bruce A. pushed off the sidewalk and skated across the street. He made two big circles in the middle of the road, then came back to where I stood.

The day was already starting to get hot. My head was hot. The smell of roses came up around me.

"Elyse." He leaned forward, close to me. "Elyse. What you saw was all a mistake."

My face wasn't doing the I-don't-care-at-all look very well now. I felt my eyes narrow and my lips go thin.

"Anna-Leigh and I have been friends for a long time. And she thinks I'm the only person who has ever been nice to her because she's, you know, fat. And then we thought about an article about not kissing too young, and I kind of disagreed with people being *too* young, and she kind of agreed that you could be too young and so we tried it ourselves." At first Bruce A. talked fast, running his words together. Then he slowed way down and separated all the words with what sounded like periods. "To see. About. It. Kissing. Too. Young. I mean."

"I've been her friend," I said, my eyes still squinchy, my lips still thin. I remembered Anna-Leigh and me laughing over a silly drawing she had done.

"Yeah, you have. But she didn't know that you and I

were hand-holding–type friends. You know, like you're more than a friend, more than a newspaper helper. She just thought that you and I are buds."

For some reason flower buds popped into my head. Maybe because I was in Mr. Clark's yard. I smiled at the thought of Bruce A. and me being like flower buds. I liked the idea.

"And then we thought about kissing. The article, I mean."

"I never saw it," I said. "I never saw the article."

"I didn't write it. Not after . . . well, you know."

I raised my eyebrows at Bruce A. and waited for him to say more. "Don't be mad at me anymore," he said. "I told her everything after you . . . after you saw us. And she said she was sorry. She was really embarrassed about the whole thing. And I was too."

"So you want me back on the paper?" I asked.

Bruce A. nodded. "But mostly I want you to . . ." He looked off into the sky, squinting one eye. "I want you to take on a little extra work for the paper. I want you to do feature articles. I've thought about this a lot, Elyse."

"It sounds like it, Bruce A.," I said. The sun made me squint too. Bruce A. looked a little soft.

"I'll think about it," I said.

"Say yes."

"No," I said.

"No, you won't be the feature writer?"

"No, I won't say yes. I'll think about it."

Bruce A. skated to the middle of the street again. "Will you come on Saturday?"

"Yeah," I said, and nodded.

Bruce A. smiled and started off toward home. He whirled around once in the road, then skated over to the stop sign on the opposite side of the street. He picked a small purple-and-white morning glory that was growing up the sign and came back to me.

"Here," he said. Then he skated away, fast, down the sidewalk.

I sighed big. The hot sun felt good on my head. It felt good all through me. I was liking today. I twirled my gift fast between my fingers, blending the white color in the throat of the flower with the purple color there. Then I turned and started in through the gate where Granny and Mr. Clark both stood watching me.

"What?" I asked. "It was a newspaper deal."

"We could see that," Mr. Clark said. And Granny laughed.

Chapter Sixteen

Private Journal of Elyse Donaldson, World-class Writer.
Ideas so far: Being buds, another strange world where peo-
ple become flowers and decide they like each other
I'm on the paper again!!!!!!!!!!

sea green

Once a month Granny went to see Dr. Brackenbury, the Alzheimer's doctor.

"I'll go with you, Granny," I told her the afternoon
Mom was going to take her to the office. "To hold
your hand. In case of you-know-what."

"Shots," Granny said.

"Yes," I said. "But don't say it out loud."

That wasn't the only reason I wanted to see Dr.
Brackenbury. He reminded me of a movie star. His
eyes were so blue they looked fake. He always had a
suntan. He spoke straight to the point with Granny,
not like Dr. Lauret, who was so gentle you'd have
thought Granny was *his* mother.

"He hasn't given me a shot yet," Granny said.

"Not that you remember," I said.

Mom picked Granny and me up and drove us the few miles to the plaza where Dr. Brackenbury's office was.

Once in his office he was quick, checking Granny's pulse and feeling her skin. He listened to her breathing and glared at me when I twisted too far on his small black stool and fell over on the floor.

"Oops," I said.

Dr. Brackenbury raised his eyebrows, then continued the exam.

"You're looking great, Mrs. Ivie," he said. "Your health is wonderful. You've even gained three pounds since coming to stay with your daughter."

"Keep going, Granny, and you could be a sumo wrestler," I said, and at that moment thought of a question for Dear Miss Know-it-all. *My brother wants to be a sumo wrestler but he's only four foot three inches and fifty-six pounds. He insists on eating all the candy in the house, trying to get fat. Can you*— I didn't have a chance to finish the thought. Dr. Brackenbury was giving me a terrible look. "Sorry," I said.

"Keep up the good work, Mrs. Donaldson," Dr. Brackenbury said. "She's looking better." And then he was out of the room and off to see someone else.

I was stunned. So stunned that at first I couldn't even move.

"Let's go, Mother," Mom said. She and Granny left.

I stood silent in the middle of the room until Mom's voice brought me down the hall after her. "Come on, Elyse, I have to get back to work."

I walked like a zombie from the office. My heart was pounding so hard I could actually feel it in my throat.

Granny was going to get better. Dr. Brackenbury had said so himself.

A few days later, when Granny and I were taking another walk, Mr. Clark met us on the sidewalk. "Hurry this way," he said, hobbling toward his yard. "I've got something to show you two."

Mr. Clark opened the gate and let Granny and me into his yard. He went over to the house and lifted the garage door. There sat an old car, the red color of Bing cherries. *Roadster* was written in silver letters near the keyhole of the trunk. I'd seen it plenty of times, whenever Mr. Clark washed it. But this was the first time that I had ever been invited to see it. Granny must have made the difference.

"Can you believe they won't let me drive this old thing?" he asked, patting the car. Granny and I shook our heads.

"It's beautiful," Granny said; then she turned to me. "Granddaddy and I had a Buick like that, only it was blue."

"What?" Mr. Clark asked. He leaned toward us a little.

"I said my husband and I had a car just like this," Granny said again, only louder this time.

Mr. Clark ran his rough hand over the shiny, flared back lights. Then he went to the front of the car and opened the door. He climbed in and turned the engine over. It started right away.

"Gotta keep the car in shape," Mr. Clark yelled. His voice echoed in the garage. "Steer clear."

Granny and I moved off to the side, as far as we could get from the driveway without standing in the garden. With a leap and a jerk, Mr. Clark backed up his car. He screeched to a halt a half inch from the fence that ran across his driveway.

"Wow," I said. But I don't think Granny heard me because now Mr. Clark was gunning the motor.

"Hop in," he hollered to us. "We'll warm up the engine."

"I don't think that's such a good idea," I said to Mr. Clark, but Granny was already on her way around the car.

"What?" Mr. Clark asked.

"Nothing," I shouted back.

I was afraid to climb in, but Granny was trying to open the door. Her arthritis was slowing her down. Maybe it would save our lives.

"I think we should head on home," I said to her over the roof of Mr. Clark's car. I wondered if he had the gas pedal pressed all the way to the floor.

"What?" Mr. Clark asked again.

"Nonsense," Granny said.

I pointed over to Granny to let Mr. Clark know that I had been talking to her. That was a mistake. He stretched across the front seat and pulled up the lock. Granny climbed into the car, slamming the door.

I wondered how badly hurt the two of them would be if Mr. Clark accidentally put the car into gear and crashed through the garage and into his living room. Then I wondered what Mom would say when she found out I'd let Granny go driving alone with an old man. I got into the car.

"Put on a seat belt," I hollered to Granny. But she didn't seem worried. In fact, she was grinning. Smoke puffed up around the windows.

"I've never been in a wreck," Mr. Clark shouted.

"I'm glad about that," I shouted back.

"What?" Mr. Clark asked.

"Nothing," I said, shaking my head. His comment made me nervous. I started looking for my own seat belt. I couldn't see one.

The roar of the engine died down to a low rumble.

"Hold on to your hat," Mr. Clark said.

"Hat?" was the only word I had the chance to get out. Mr. Clark put the car in drive and screeched into the garage. He slammed the brakes on hard, throwing me to the floor and onto my knees. I was just high enough to see over the front seat. Granny jerked forward but she didn't fly into the windshield the way I expected. I pushed myself back up into a sitting position. Before I could say another word Mr. Clark had the car in reverse. We whipped down the driveway again. I didn't even have time to look and see if we were going to hit the fence. Screech, jerk, halt, roar. Four times Mr. Clark drove in and out of the garage. I held on tight, praying I wouldn't get whiplash. My teeth snapped together again and again. I felt glad Mom was dating a dentist.

Mr. Clark pulled into the garage, and after roaring the engine for an entire deafening minute, he turned the car off. He smiled at Granny, then back at me. Perhaps he needed to visit Dr. Brackenbury too.

"Granny?" I said, to see if she was all right. This would make a great journal entry. *Today Mr. Clark tried to kill me in his car.* It sounded like a mystery.

Granny touched her hair like she was checking to see if it was still in place. She smiled at Mr. Clark. How had she stayed in the front seat? I heard a seat belt snap open. We all got out.

"Can you believe they won't let me drive this old thing?" Mr. Clark asked again, smoothing his hand over the car as he shut the door with a soft click.

I looked wide-eyed at him to see if he was kidding. He wasn't. Granny shook her head, her face solemn. I nodded. *Thank goodness for the driving bureau,* I wanted to sing out. *You've saved the country from Mr. Clark, driveway speed demon.*

"I miss driving," Mr. Clark said. We walked to the garden, Mr. Clark casting sad glances back at his cherry-red car.

Once in the garden Granny seemed to feel at home. With effort she knelt with Mr. Clark, and they began to talk about weeds and insects and the biggest things they had ever grown and when potato bugs had done lots of damage.

I tuned them out. I felt nervous after Mr. Clark's wild ride. *He could be a Disney attraction,* I thought. I turned my head left and right to make sure my neck still worked. Then I sat at the end of one row and began pulling new weeds from the earth. The dirt felt good on my skin. Working in the garden made me relax. After a little bit the shaking stopped.

Dear Miss Know-it-all, I thought. *My grandfather drives like a bat out of—hmmm, what would be a good word?— Hades. How can we stop him? Signed, Driving Me Crazy. . . . Dear Driving Me Crazy, Cut the brake lines.*

I started to giggle about Mr. Clark's car ride and Dear Miss Know-it-all. The sun pounded down hot on me and it was only a few minutes before I was really sweating.

"Women perspire and men sweat," I remembered Granny saying once when I had told her I was sweating like a pig.

"Please, Elyse," Granny had said. "Act like the little lady you are."

I was thinking about the differences in sweat and wondering just how much control I had over it when Patrick and Caleb rode up. They parked their bikes on the sidewalk and came close to the fence.

"Look who's helping the old geezer today," Patrick said. Caleb sneered.

I was glad that Mr. Clark's fence separated us from them, glad I was protected by grapevines and rose-bushes. My movements all of a sudden felt jerky and exaggerated. I wondered if they could see that I was afraid. I wondered if Granny would mind me sweating like a pig now.

"Hey, ugly," Caleb said in a loud voice. "Are these old people the only friends you can find?"

"They're probably baby-sitting her," Patrick said, and he laughed like what he had said was funny.

I kept on digging, my fingers finding the bottoms of weeds and pulling them out.

"You look better playing in the dirt," Caleb said. "It's doing wonders for your skin. It's covering you up so no one has to look at you."

I didn't know what to do. Patrick and Caleb never talked to me when I was with anyone. They always picked on me when I was alone. Having Granny and Mr. Clark there made the words even more embarrassing.

"Leave me alone," I said. The nice feeling was gone from the morning. Now I was burning up in the hot sun and the dirt was gritty on my skin.

"Did you say something to me?" Patrick asked, and his voice sounded all ugly.

I didn't answer.

"Your mother should have killed you at birth," he said. It was then that a spray of water hit him in the neck.

It arced silver over my head, spreading in a wide burst that soaked both Patrick and Caleb. It hit them in the chest and face and pants. They stumbled, trying to get away, backing into their bikes, nearly falling. A fine mist fell on me, cooling my skin. I felt like I sat under a rainbow.

I looked toward Granny. Mr. Clark stood with his feet apart like a gunfighter from an old Western. He walked through his garden, pulling the hose at his side, water gun aimed forward.

Patrick and Caleb cursed and shouted, and when they did, Mr. Clark shot water in their mouths. At last they ran, pushing their bikes until they could jump onto them, and pedaled away. Mr. Clark soaked their backs good.

He turned then and looked to where I sat opened-mouthed. Water dripped from the nozzle of the hose.

"This is one of my favorite garden tools," he said. And Granny clapped.

Chapter Seventeen

Private Journal of Elyse Donaldson, World-class Writer.
Ideas so far: !!Miracle Cures!!, cleaning our streets with
water (Patrick and Caleb thing) and washing the bullies
away (Patrick and Caleb thing)   Mr. Clark is so
cool, but he's not a very good driver.

eucalyptus

Saturday morning I woke up hot in the sunroom. The entire room was golden with light and heat. Today would be a scorcher, I could tell. I stretched out long on the sofa bed, curling and uncurling my toes, pulling my arms up over my head, trying to crack my back.

Jordyn came in. "Elyse, there's somebody here to see you."

My heart skipped a beat. Was it Bruce A.? Maybe he was over to pick me up.

"Tell him to hold on," I said.

Jordyn kind of cocked her head, then shrugged and left.

I got dressed in shorts and an old shirt as fast as I could, then ran out barefoot into the living room.

Anna-Leigh was waiting for me, her arms crossed over her stomach, her pink pants stretched tight over her legs.

"Oh," I said.

"Hi, Elyse," she said. She moved a hand through her thick dark hair and I noticed she had polished her nails a color that reminded me of a storm. "I wanted to walk over to Bruce's house with you."

"I know the way," I said.

Anna-Leigh looked at the carpet and scuffed her foot against it. "I know," she said. "I just want to talk. Since we'll be working together again."

I stood silent for a minute. I didn't know quite what to say. It was easy to not like Anna-Leigh when she was standing in my memory, pressed against Bruce A. It wasn't so easy to not like her when she was standing in my living room, obviously sorry.

I nodded and then motioned to her. "I still have to eat," I said. "You want to join me?"

"I'll watch," she said, "and talk to you."

I made myself a bowl of cereal and sat down at the kitchen table. Anna-Leigh sat across from me.

"Your house is nice," she said.

I blinked. "No it isn't," I said. "It's shabby and old."

"All the houses around here are shabby and old," she said. "But the colors your mom's chosen. They make this place seem, umm, comfortable."

"I've never noticed," I said. I glanced around the kitchen, a sunny yellow color, with crisp yellow-and-white-checked curtains. Mom had decorated the walls with old cooking things, like an ancient corn bread pan and a bunch of cookie presses. To me this was home, nothing special. I tried to see it through Anna-Leigh's eyes. It did look comfortable and kind of happy, even.

"What's your house look like?" I asked.

"My dad's been remodeling it ever since I was born. He doesn't have a lot of time. Not with working at Geneva Steel. It's always in some stage of repair. It gets on my nerves."

I finished my cereal, then made my way into the bathroom to brush my teeth and wash my face. Anna-Leigh waited for me in the living room.

"I didn't know," she said when I walked back in to get her so we could start over to Bruce A.'s place.

"What?"

"That you and Bruce were, you know, friends."

I felt all my blood rush to my face. "What do you mean?"

"That day you came in," Anna-Leigh said, and she crossed her arms in front of herself again. "We really were doing research for the paper."

"Oh."

"And I'm sorry to have hurt your feelings."

"It's okay," I said. And it was by then. This morning's visit and the invitation to work again on the paper had made things right. "Let's go."

Outside, the July sun was hot, even this early in the morning. I breathed deep the feeling of having two good friends and started the walk with Anna-Leigh to Bruce A.'s house.

"Elyse," Nosy Nikki called. She stood on her front porch, her white hair tied up in a crazy leopard bandanna. "How's your grandmother?"

"Getting better," I said. "Getting lots better."

"I've been up all night. I couldn't sleep a wink," Nosy Nikki said. "I can't believe how tired I am. That's what happens when you get old."

"All right," I said, and hurried away from her with Anna-Leigh.

"I love your little paper," Nosy Nikki called. "Those horoscopes have been right on, every time."

"I'm glad," I said, and waved.

Anna-Leigh looked at me. "Don't you make those things up?"

"Yes," I said. "But maybe I have a new career goal now."

The work on this edition, four pages because it was a special one, took a lot of time. I had already completed my horoscopes for the week and written a few extra Dear Miss Know-it-alls and even done one nice story about how great most of the neighborhood was, so I didn't have to worry about that.

As soon as we walked into his bedroom, Bruce A. handed me a small stack of papers. "These need to be edited," he said. "I've looked at that stuff so much I think I'm going crazy."

We worked hard that whole morning.

This is good, I thought, stretching back on the bed while I went through the editing stuff. Jordyn and Mom weren't the only people in the family who actually had friends. I did too. I liked the way it felt. I liked being with Bruce A. and Anna-Leigh.

Is this what it felt like for Mom to be with Dr. Lauret? Did she get a funny flip-flop feeling in her stomach when she saw him, like I did when I saw Bruce A.? Did she feel all breathy when Dr. Lauret accidentally brushed her arm with his?

Better yet, did Anna-Leigh? I could see by looking into her eyes when she talked to Bruce A. that she liked him a lot. Did she feel all the same things I did?

Probably. And still I liked her. I liked being with her, laughing at the funny things she said. It took a lot of guts for her to work with me and to apologize to me and to still be my friend. I liked her for that.

We finished work on the paper by noon and ate

lunch with Bruce A. and all his brothers and sisters. It was a loud lunch but it was fun.

Then I set off for home. I nearly ran into Patrick and Caleb, but by sneaking through a bunch of back-yards I was able to get home safe and sound.

That's when I got the surprise of my life. Mom was standing in the middle of the living room with Jordyn, wearing a dress. Whoever heard of wearing a dress on a Saturday afternoon?

That's what I said.

I came walking up the stairs and caught Mom twirling around the living room in a past-her-knees shiny peach-colored dress.

"Elyse?" Mom said. "What do you think?" And she swirled around again. The dress billowed out from her body and I could see Mom's slender legs as she turned.

"Whoever heard of wearing a dress on a Saturday afternoon?" I asked. The dress looked beautiful on Mom. I mean, *she* looked beautiful. A yucky feeling crept into my stomach.

"Maggie brought it down for me when she came to pick up Mother this morning," Mom said, and she smoothed her hands down the material of the dress like it felt especially good to her fingers.

"Mom," Jordyn said, "I'll fix your hair up so you can show off your neck. You'll look terrific."

One of Mom's hands reached up to her throat like she was surprised she even had one. My yucky feeling grew stronger.

"When are you going to wear it?" I asked. "I think it's a bit much for the dentist's office, don't you?"

"I'm going dancing tonight," Mom said. "With Michael."

"Michael?"

"You know," Jordyn said, "Dr. Lauret."

"Dancing?" I asked. "Dancing with a dentist?" It sounded like the title of a movie or something.

Mom blushed a little, then nodded. "If Aunt Maggie wasn't watching Mother tonight, she'd come too, with Jared."

"You're going dancing in a dress like that?"

She nodded again.

"What music do they have for old people to dance to? Those big bands like on Lawrence Welk?" I said all this knowing Mom dances around our house, like a kid, to the music Jordyn and I listen to. And I know she only lets Lawrence Welk be turned on because Granny likes watching those old reruns.

Mom forced a smile. "We're not going to do this again, Elyse. I'm not going to let you ruin tonight for me."

"*Me* ruin something for *you*?" I shouted.

Mom squinched her eyes up small.

"Don't act like a jerk," Jordyn said.

"Great," I said. "You gang up on me too."

All of a sudden Mom was a peach blur. In just a few steps she was right in my face. "Elyse Donaldson, you listen to me and you listen with both ears."

I had no choice; she was in my space, good and solid. She could have worked on my teeth if I had opened my mouth. I didn't.

"I like Michael Lauret. I will go out with him. Do you understand? Now let me be." Mom turned then, fast, and the dress whirled out, showing a pair of white shorts underneath. Mom stomped down the hall and slammed her door.

"Gol," I said, "how immature." I looked over at Jordyn, who stood with her hands on her hips. "Mom needs to grow up. Dating is making her act like a baby."

Jordyn rolled her eyes. Then she kind of slumped into Granny's empty rocker.

"Elyse, Mom has to have a life of her own," she said, and her voice sounded deflated.

"She has a life," I said. "You, me, Granny."

"That's not a life. It's only a partial life. She's always taking care of someone. She needs a chance to live."

"She's living," I said, not listening to my sister because there was a stubborn lump filling up my heart.

Jordyn shook her head then and went off down the hall to Mom's room. I heard her knock, then heard Mom's door open and shut.

"Fine!" I screamed. "Fine. Ruin a perfect day. You both always do this to me."

I ran then, down to the sunroom. Slamming the door behind me, I leaped onto my bed. A spring jabbed me in the ribs but I ignored the pain and beat my pillow with my fists.

Why does she have to do this? I thought. *She has me and Jordyn and Granny.*

A thought started to creep into my brain. I did my best to ignore it, but I couldn't keep it out at all.

You have Anna-Leigh, the thought said. *And Bruce A. And Mr. Clark.*

"Shut up," I said to the thought. "Just shut up."

But it was too late. I realized it was all true. I did have people in my life. Friends. Things to do other than just watch Granny and sit around.

And what did Mom have? Yeah, me and Jordyn. Granny, who needed to be taken care of. A job.

I tried to remember Mom doing anything fun for herself and I couldn't think of any times at all except when Aunt Maggie came down and took her out to dinner.

"Until now," I said out loud to my pillow. "Now she has Dr. Dancing Dentist Michael Lauret."

I rolled onto my back and sat up. I looked around my room. It was a mess. In one corner was a pile of my clothes. There were papers all over the floor near my desk. My books were scattered near my shelf and next to the bed. There was a row of dirty glasses lining a windowsill.

Mom had kept her bargain with me. She hadn't come into this room and rolled her eyes even once. She hadn't asked me to clean up. She was giving me a work-free bedroom for the summer.

She just wants a friend, the thought said. *Like Bruce A.*

"Bigger than Bruce A.," I said.

I remembered Mom, tired after work, coming in and starting dinner. I remembered her sitting early in the morning with Granny, trying to get her to eat. Mom worked hard. I'd never really noticed before. It was a weird feeling I was having right at that very moment.

She did need time. She did need . . . I couldn't make myself say it, so instead I went and sat at my desk with a crayon in one hand and tried to write a story about a girl who set her mother free, but nothing more would come to me than the idea.

Chapter Eighteen

Private Journal of Elyse Donaldson, World-class Writer.
Ideas so far: Arguing with parents   Mom really likes
Dr. Lauret. I don't get why things have to change so
much. She had a good time at the dance, and I caught her
kissing him again. I didn't flash the porch light this time,
though, and when she finally came in I told her I was sorry
for acting like a jerk.

fuchsia

A few days later Granny and I passed Mr. Clark's house on our early-morning walk. I wasn't surprised to see his garden in ruins. Granny and I stood silent inside his fence, watching him as he knelt in the mess of destroyed plants that were wilting in the sun.

"Maybe I can help," I said to Granny, but she shook her head. I walked over and squatted beside Mr. Clark. I picked up a broken stick and tried to tie the slender stem of a crushed tomato plant to it. It bent in half, the leaves brushing the ground. I moved to the next plant and tied it up too. And the next, and the next.

"Elyse," said Mr. Clark, and I looked over at him. "It's no use. They're dead. We can't save them."

"I hate those guys," I said. "I hate them for doing this." I wanted to make sure Mr. Clark heard me, so I said it again, really loud this time. I waved my arms out wide, showing that I meant the whole garden and Patrick and Caleb. Guilt crept under my skin, coloring it. This had happened because of me. If I hadn't been in Mr. Clark's garden . . .

"This is my fault," I said.

"Get real," Jordyn said. She was standing next to Granny. When had she come up? "Those jerks did it. Not you."

The sun was high enough to shine in my face when I looked up. I shaded my eyes with my hand. It smelled like tomato plants.

"They did it because I was here," I said, embarrassed.

Jordyn turned from me to Mr. Clark. "You need to call the police," she said. "You need to report this."

"I can't prove anything," Mr. Clark said. "It happened late in the night, I guess. It was like this when I came out here."

"The police should know," Jordyn said. "They need to know the cause. At least who you think did it."

Granny shook her head. "It was that nasty hail," she said.

"What?" Jordyn and I said at the same time.

"All that hail this morning. The crop is ruined." Tears began to run down Granny's cheeks, catching rides on the wrinkles and dripping from her chin.

"How will we live this year with the entire field devastated?"

I looked to Mr. Clark, who suddenly seemed to have perfect hearing. He walked to Granny, trying not to step on any of the garden.

"Pa," Granny said when Mr. Clark came close to us. "Whatever will we do?" She leaned on Mr. Clark's shoulder and began to sob.

I was mortified. My tongue went dry in my mouth. Granny was acting ridiculous in an almost complete stranger's yard. In fact, she was bawling on his left front breast pocket. I opened my mouth a couple of times but I couldn't think of anything to say.

"Let's take her home," Jordyn said, and she walked over to Granny.

Mr. Clark continued to pat Granny on the back. "It's okay, Grace," he said. I don't know about Granny, but the softness of his voice made me feel better.

"Come on, Granny," Jordyn said. "Let's go home."

"I'm lost," Granny said. "I'm staying right here in the fields till someone can come and find me."

"I've found you, Grace," Mr. Clark said. "You're not lost anymore. Let's go inside and have some iced tea. I think it'll make you feel better."

Granny looked up at Mr. Clark and began a fresh burst of crying.

"Pa," she said, over and over again.

Mr. Clark guided Granny toward his house.

"What do we do?" I asked Jordyn.

"Follow them, I guess," she said.

We picked our way through the broken garden to the back steps, where Mr. Clark helped Granny into his kitchen. The room was cool and dark after the bright light outside. Mr. Clark pulled out a chair for Granny to sit on and then went to the fridge and got out a pitcher of tea. He set it on the table and got four glasses out of the cabinet and then came and sat down with us.

"Here, Grace," he said to Granny, swirling the tea around the glass pitcher before pouring her some. I saw the melted sugar rise from the bottom like an upside-down tornado. "This will make you feel better."

Granny took the drink and sipped at it. "Johnny," she said, "this is perfect. You always make the best tea."

Oh no. Now Granny thought Mr. Clark was Granddaddy. I felt my face turn red again.

"And you've let the kitchen get into a mess." Granny looked over at Jordyn and me. "He's pretty helpless when it comes to cleaning up." I remembered Granny saying that about Granddaddy lots of times before he died. It seemed strange to hear it now.

155

Granny drank her tea and every once in a while "tsked" at the dishes in Mr. Clark's sink. He just grinned. Jordyn looked around the room, which was painted a pale green, like she didn't notice anything wrong was happening. I was nervous, though. What would Granny do next?

I had barely thought the question when Granny stood and gathered our half-filled glasses of tea. She took Mr. Clark's out of his hand right as he was lifting it to his mouth to drink.

"I hate it when Addie leaves me to do all the work," she said, carrying the glasses from the table to the kitchen counter. She started water running into the sink and began to search for dish detergent. She looked in the fridge, then in the broom closet and twice in the oven. She pulled open a few drawers. At last she found it sitting on the windowsill. It had been staring her right in the face the whole time. I looked away from my grandmother.

"It's not her fault," Mr. Clark said, and he motioned toward Granny with a tilt of his head. He was talking to both Jordyn and me but I didn't look at him. I kept my head down, my hair hiding my face. At least I hoped it was hiding my face. "She can't help it, you know."

"She has Alzheimer's," Jordyn said.

I rubbed my fingertips on the table. It was golden

and smooth, almost warm. Maybe if I concentrated hard I could pretend that I wasn't here. Pretend my granny wasn't acting strange. Pretend the garden was better. Pretend I wasn't feeling so embarrassed.

It seemed all I did anymore was spend my free time feeling embarrassed. Embarrassed about my looks, about my mother dating a divorced dancing dentist, about the way Patrick and Caleb treated me and now about Granny. It took a lot of energy to be this embarrassed all the time.

"I don't care what you call it," Mr. Clark said. "I just know it's not her fault." He paused, then reached over and tapped the table under my nose.

"What?" I asked, looking sideways out of my eyes without really turning my head.

"It's not your fault either, Elyse. You're not responsible for the way other people act. All you need to do is love her the way she is."

"Sometimes I don't know her," I told Mr. Clark. I saw Jordyn nod in agreement, her hair swinging near her face.

Mr. Clark nodded too. "I don't know any of the medical mumbo jumbo. All I know is that your grandmother is scared too. And so you love her up, no matter what happens. You'll be a lot happier. Somehow loving people makes things easier. At least it always has for me."

I glanced over at Granny, who stood washing dishes and talking to herself. She turned and looked straight at me.

"Come help me with these dishes, Addie," she said. "It was your chore in the first place."

I stole a look at Mr. Clark and he smiled big. I wondered for a second if his teeth were real. They sure didn't look it. The gums were way too pink. Maybe Dr. Lauret could help.

"Addie," Granny said. "I'm waiting."

Embarrassed at being called Addie in front of Mr. Clark and Jordyn, I pushed myself away from the table and walked over to Granny.

"It's about time," she said, and handed me a dishrag. "You dry. I'm almost finished, and since you didn't get here in time to do your share, you can throw the dirty water to the chickens."

I stood quiet and dried the dishes. Mr. Clark was right. Granny didn't want to be this way. I had seen her sitting sad in our living room I don't know how many times. I knew she knew something was happening to her, even if she wasn't quite sure what it was.

Granny's flower smell mingled with the mountain-fresh-air smell of the soap and tingled in my nose. For some reason I felt sad and the tingling got my eyes to watering. Great, now I was going to cry right here at the sink in Mr. Clark's house. Why couldn't I do that at home in bed instead of in public?

I felt sad for all the awful things in my world.

Poor old me. Poor old Granny. Poor old Mr. Clark. Poor old Mr. Clark's garden.

I looked over at Jordyn. She still sat at the table, her chin resting in her hand. No way did I feel sorry for her. She had everything going for her.

A slow, fat tear slid out of the corner of one of my eyes and trickled its way down near the side of my nose. I wiped it away with the drying cloth.

Well, at least I wasn't feeling embarrassed anymore.

Chapter Nineteen

Private Journal of Elyse Donaldson, World-class Writer. Ideas so far: Sabotage and the alien bullies taking over the neighborhood of Northwest Orem   I've planned to love Granny for who she is and try not to feel so embarrassed when she does something crazy like yell out the bathroom window that I've kidnapped her.

red violet

Mom called us in for a morning family meeting. Granny was still sleeping. It was early. Mom and Jordyn sat at the foot of my bed. Both of them looked fresh and pretty. I could hardly open my eyes.

"School starts in a month, girls," Mom said.

"Oh yuck," I said. I turned onto my stomach so I wouldn't have to think about it. A month. I breathed my own breath in and out a couple of times. That was as bad as school starting. I turned over again.

"Sit up, honey," Mom said, squeezing my foot.

"Oh, please don't make me. I'll keep my eyes open, I promise. But right now my body is still too tired to bend."

"Okay," Mom said. "But this is important. Don't go to sleep."

"I won't," I said, and forced my eyes open. I needed a couple of toothpicks, like the cartoon characters use, as props for my eyelids.

"School starts in a month," Mom said again. "And we need to decide what we're going to do with Granny."

"I've been thinking about that," said Jordyn.

"What do you mean?" I asked. It was a miracle! I could bend *and* sit up. My eyes had no problem staying wide open. "She'll stay here, won't she?"

"There'd be no one to stay home with her," Mom said. "I can't quit work and you girls will be in class."

"That's not fair," I said.

"Mom's right, though," said Jordyn. "You know Granny can't be left alone. Some days are good for her. Some aren't."

"I know," I said. "But I could stay with her. You know, home school."

Mom blinked twice, surprised. "No," she said. "Anyway, there's a place a few blocks away from here. It's kind of like a home—"

"Mom," I said, my voice a little louder than I meant it to be. "You promised Granny she'd never go into an old folks' home. You even made me promise not to do it to you."

"Relax, Elyse," Mom said. "This is a place just for Alzheimer's patients. There are not a lot of people living there. Each patient gets his or her own room. And we're close enough that the two of you could get Granny on your way home from school if you wanted."

"But, Mom," I said. "You promised her."

"Yeah, Mom," said Jordyn. "Granny doesn't want to waste away to nothing in a rest home. She's told me that lots of times."

Mom sighed big. "Girls, I understand your concern. But this is my dilemma: Granny cannot stay home alone. She might burn the place down, she might wander away and get hit by a car, she might fall and break a hip and we wouldn't know until three-twenty when you two came home. Is that what you want?"

Both Jordyn and I shook our heads.

"Who will work if I stay home with Granny?"

I shrugged. I felt like I was riding a yo-yo. My feelings went up and down with everything Mom or Jordyn said. I knew Granny couldn't be alone, but I hated to not keep Mom's word to her.

Jordyn looked wide-eyed. "I guess I could get a job after school," she said.

"No," Mom said. "I don't want you to do that. I still think you're a little young. And you'd never make the amount of money I make. We need to look at things from this point of view: Granny cannot live alone. I cannot stay home with her. Neither can either of you. That leaves us only two choices. A rest home or this place I heard about that's not too far from here."

"My vote," said Jordyn, "is the place you're talking about. We already promised not to send Granny to an old folks' home."

"Good," Mom said. "I'm glad we agree. Now, I've made an appointment for us to go over and see this place after I get home from work. Have Granny ready, and, Elyse, I want you in something clean. Don't wear that same pair of shorts and that raggedy T-shirt another day. And please do your hair. Maybe we'll like this place. Maybe we won't. But let's hope that we do, because if not, our options become severely limited."

Jordyn and I nodded.

"There's a big fence around the place," I said as soon as we got to Aspen Manor.

"I see it," said Mom. We had walked over the five blocks from our house and now we were standing outside a tall gate. A little sign said RING BUZZER. Mom pushed a tiny white button.

"I only see *three* aspen trees. And they're pretty scrawny at that."

"Elyse," Granny said. "Give this place a chance."

I was surprised. I knew she and Mom had had a talk about this. And I knew it had gone well because Mom had said so. But for Granny to be this positive? Granny seemed to sense my question. "I'm going to need help," she said.

Mom pressed the buzzer again and a window in the front of the building slid open. A redheaded lady stuck her face to the screen. "Just push the gate when you press the buzzer," she shouted at us. Mom did and the gate opened. A hand from the window waved at us and then pointed toward a door at the front of the building.

A pretty lady, tiny like Granny but not so old, was waiting for us.

"Come in, come in," she said. "Let me show you around."

"I'm Mrs. Donaldson," Mom said. "This is my mother, Grace Ivie."

The lady shook hands with Mom and Granny.

"And who are these pretty girls?" she asked. Mom introduced Jordyn and me.

"Let me show you around," said the little lady. "We have running water." She pointed to a water fountain in the corner. "Go ahead and taste it," she said to me. "It's cold."

"That's okay," I said. "We have the same kind at school."

"No, really," she said, "I want your opinion."

"In a little bit," Mom said.

164

The lady smiled a big smile at me. "We have all the modern conveniences," she said. "Over there is the kitchen. Always clean. No roaches. We don't allow roaches in here."

"I'm glad about that," said Granny.

"I didn't catch your name," Mom said to our helper.

"It's Jasmine," the lady said. "Princess Jasmine."

Granny's eyes got big but Mom never missed a beat.

"Well, Jasmine," she said, "I'm looking for Brittany Walker. Do you know where her office is?"

"Oh yes," the lady said. "Let me show you."

Princess Jasmine? I thought. I wanted to laugh so I wouldn't feel so tense inside, but I couldn't. My laugher had stopped working.

"Don't forget to try that water before you leave," Princess Jasmine said.

"We won't," Jordyn said. We followed Jasmine down a long hall to the office. Mom tapped at the door.

It swung open and there stood a chubby lady in black stretch pants and a flowered shirt. Her red hair was caught back in a barrette.

"Beth," she said to Jasmine, "I see you were the welcome lady today. Thank you."

"I'm Jasmine," the little lady said.

"Oh, okay."

As Beth walked away Brittany Walker said, "She's a different flower every day."

Mom smiled but Granny looked worried.

Brittany Walker showed us the "facilities." The bedrooms were small but neat. The people who lived here had decorated their places the way they wanted. The kitchen was clean. I searched for roaches anyway. I couldn't see any. There was a big cafeterialike room with round tables and a huge window that looked out onto a large grassy yard. I saw an aspen tree there that I hadn't noticed when we were in the front of the building. There was a TV room with a big-screen television and a recreation room that had a lot of chairs lining the walls, and a piano. On the wall was a calendar that told all the activities for the month.

"Look, Granny," said Jordyn. "Low-impact aerobics. Every Tuesday and Thursday."

"And arts-and-crafts day is on Monday afternoons, and that night you can go to a country-and-western dance class," I said.

The calendar was loaded with things to do. It sounded like fun, although it was hard for me to picture Jasmine doing the swing or the two-step-shuffle country-and-western dances I learned in P.E. during the winter months when we couldn't get out because there was too much snow. My hands always sweat then and sometimes I had to be the boy because I was so tall. It was embarrassing. Of course, Granny wouldn't have any trouble with the tall part. But I did wonder if her hands would sweat. I mean *perspire*.

At the end of the tour Brittany Walker said, "We can only have twenty-five residents. We don't want things to get too big here. We want to be able to work easily with the residents. If you're interested, I have paperwork for you to fill out."

Mom looked at Granny, who nodded. "This is a nice place," Granny said. Mom took the papers.

As we walked out the door, Jasmine-Beth stopped us. "Did you try the water?" she asked.

"No, but I will," Mom said. She took a big drink. "Oh, it's cold. And good, too." We each sipped at the water, saying things like "Oooh" and "Aaah" and "Yummy."

"Funny," said the old lady, "I thought it tasted a bit like pee." She walked off, shaking her head.

The four of us stood silent a moment, staring bug-eyed at each other. Then Granny started to laugh. Somehow it triggered the giggles in me and I was able to laugh too. Thank goodness my laugher wasn't broken after all.

Chapter Twenty

Private Journal of Elyse Donaldson, World-class Writer. Ideas so far: Losing your favorite grandmother to a residential place for Alzheimer's patients   Granny doesn't seem too upset, but I think a part of me is crumbling away.

vivid tangerine

On Friday evening we all went clothes shopping for school. Granny, quiet, pushed the cart around K Mart. She couldn't quite remember where she was, but she followed us, humming songs I didn't recognize.

"Why I am buying you more school clothes I will never know," Mom said to me. We were looking at the twenty-five-percent-off rack. "You have more than you need already."

"To tell you the truth, Mom," I said, "most of that stuff piled in the corner I've outgrown. I could save us all time and money if you'd buy me a few pair of Levi's and some T-shirts."

"That's not the style," Jordyn said. "Don't you want

to be in style?" She was flipping fast through the clothes.

"If I looked like you, maybe," I said. "But I am most comfortable in jeans and a T-shirt."

The argument felt good. It was a peaceful one. Not like before Granny came, when I would have wanted to tear Jordyn's hair out of her head with a swift jerk. We were friends and I liked it.

"You're just a taller version of me," Jordyn said.

"Yeah, right," I said. I laughed a little. So I wasn't as pretty as my sister. That was finally okay by me. I would become a writer. A world-class writer. I would live on an island with mango trees right outside my window so I could pick them whenever I wanted, and when I was rich and famous . . .

I looked up from my little daydream to see my mother and sister and grandmother staring at me.

"Was I talking out loud or something?" I asked.

"I'm dead serious," Jordyn said. "You and I look an awful lot alike."

I opened my eyes up wide and nodded like I believed her. "The 'awful' part is true."

"Look," Jordyn said, and she directed me by the shoulders to a tall thin mirror.

"What," I said, not wanting to look, not wanting to see what I already knew.

"I said, 'Look.'" Jordyn gestured at our images.

"So?"

"So. See our hair? It's the same color. Only difference is that mine's longer."

When had my hair lightened? I wondered.

"And we have the same eye color, too."

"You're right," I said, surprised.

"Our faces are even the same shape," Jordyn said. "We look like sisters."

"You have bosoms, though," I said, pointing at our reflections.

"You'll get some," Jordyn said.

"And your nose is smaller than mine."

"What?" Jordyn asked, looking hard at the mirror and turning her head sideways. "No way."

Mom laughed.

"Now on to school supplies," I said when we had each picked out a few new things. I had decided to go ahead and stick with jeans and T-shirts.

"You girls go on," Mom said. "I want to put some things on layaway. Take Granny with you."

"All right, Mom," said Jordyn, and the three of us started off.

The best part of school starting, for me, is getting all the notebooks and paper and stuff. There's something rich about having a lot of paper and pencils in my desk at home. I looked over the shelves, imagining what I would do if I had a lot of money.

My stomach was doing flip-flops. Already it was time for school to begin. Where had the summer gone? I wasn't ready to go back. I wanted to keep working on *The Northwest Orem Gazette*. I didn't want to go back to being indoors all the time again, didn't want to have to worry if I'd have any classes with Anna-Leigh and Bruce A., or if I'd have to face Patrick and Caleb.

At least I didn't have to feel concerned about Granny. Mom had gotten her signed up at Aspen Manor. She would move in the weekend before we went to school. And like Mom had promised, on our way home in the afternoons we could get Granny, and then drop her off again at night. Granny would take turns spending weekends with us and Aunt Maggie. I thought about all this while I looked at the stocked shelves. The smell of chocolates drifted over from the next aisle. My stomach rumbled. I felt hungry.

I gathered a few packages of paper and held them up next to my body. Some pencils, a few ballpoint pens. *I'd like some stickers,* I thought, even though I was probably way too old for them. I'd never take any to school, just save them in my desk. And a few little notepads, but Mom wouldn't let me get those because they were so expensive. Tape, glue, brads, rubber bands, a few glue sticks, markers (thick and thin tips), a new package of 120 crayons and, since I was dreaming, construction paper, poster paints and poster board . . .

"Where's Granny?" Jordyn asked.

. . . three-by-five-inch cards—colored ones, lined and unlined. In my mind I was strolling through the aisle, placing whatever I wanted in a basket that was brimming with school supplies.

"Granny," Jordyn called, and I looked up.

Granny was gone.

I started after my sister as she hurried down the aisle, paper and pens under one arm.

Oh no. Mom had told me how someone with Alzheimer's had wandered away and drowned in a baby pool. Granted, there were no filled pools here at K Mart, but there was the parking lot. If Granny was confused . . .

We turned and started the search for our grandmother.

She was on the floor in the next aisle, eating peanut clusters. All around her were packages of candy, some unopened, most with a bite or two taken from them. Our cart was piled high with Dolly Madison cakes. Three of the shelves were bare, except for the cashew section. I wondered why Granny had left the cashews. And how had she worked so fast?

"Oh, Granny," Jordyn said. Then she turned to me.

"Elyse, we have to put all this food and candy away. They're going to kick us out of K Mart."

I set my school supplies on the ground and started putting things back up on the shelves. Jordyn worked beside me.

"I can't believe we let this happen," I said, putting packages of Ding Dongs where they should be. "What do you think Mr. Clark would say about this?"

"What's Mom gonna say, is more like it," Jordyn answered. "Look at all those opened things. How are we going to pay for it all?"

"I hadn't thought of that." I knelt next to Granny to save any unopened packages.

"Come on," Jordyn said after we had cleared up what we could and put what Mom was going to have to buy into the cart. "Let's get out of here."

"Come on, Granny," I said, leaning over to help her up. "Let's go find Mom." While I was trying to get Granny to her feet I wrestled a package of pink mints from her hand.

"Ow," she said when I finally got them away. "Let me alone. I'm busy."

"We've got to go."

"I'm staying here to mind the bazaar table," Granny said. "I get free tastes of everything." She winked at me. At last I had her on her feet.

"Hurry up," said Jordyn. She turned the corner with the basket.

I touched Granny on the arm. Someone announced a blue-light special. "We have to hurry," I said. When she wouldn't follow but lingered near the candies, I pulled her along as gently as I could.

"Don't you try and get fresh with me," Granny said.

"What?" I asked, my voice going up high. "Granny, that's gross." I pulled on her arm again.

Granny wouldn't budge.

I moved behind her and circled my arms around her waist.

"I'm being kidnapped," Granny shouted, her thin high voice cutting through the cool K Mart air. "I'm being kidnapped."

I moved back around to look at Granny, my face turning bright red.

There was chewed-up Ding Dong in her mouth. It made her tongue and teeth look dark brown. I looked away from my grandmother and tried to steer her away and toward Mom, wherever that was. "Come on, Mom's waiting for us."

"Momma always said Spanish Fork isn't as safe as it seems," Granny called out to a little boy and his mother.

My face turned even redder. *Granny can't help this,* I said to myself. *She doesn't mean it.*

Jordyn hurried back to where I was. "Let's go," she said.

"I'm trying to," I said. "Why don't you help me? I can't do it all alone."

Jordyn moved close and together we led Granny back toward where Mom had said she'd be. K Mart had never seemed so big.

"I'm being stolen by complete strangers," Granny called. "This is a kidnapping. Won't anyone here help me?" People stared as we worked our way through the Friday-night crowd.

We went past the flashing light of the blue-light special.

"Officer," Granny said, grabbing a chubby man dressed in green coveralls who was going through the rakes and hoes. "Officer. Please. I'm being kidnapped. Won't you help me?"

The light went around and around. "Just five minutes left on the garden-tools sale at the center of the store," a voice said over the intercom.

Why did we have to come to K Mart on a Friday night? I thought. *This is so embarrassing.*

The chubby man let go of the hoe he had in his hand.

"Do you know these two girls?" he asked Granny.

Granny began to cry. "No, Officer," she said. "I was minding the sample table at the bazaar and they came up and took me away. Please get me home."

"This is our grandmother," Jordyn said. Her face was red and her voice didn't seem to be working. "She has Alzheimer's." Jordyn whispered this part. I nodded.

"I see," said the chubby man. "My father had that." He took Granny's arm. She leaned into him, wiping the tears that ran down her face onto his shirt. I prayed she wouldn't try to blow her nose there as well.

"Are you here alone?" he asked Jordyn.

"No sir. Our mom is supposed to be at the layaway counter."

The man led Granny around the store, up and down the aisles toward Layaway. Much to my relief, Mom was waiting in a line there.

"This is your daughter, ma'am," the man said to Granny after I pointed out Mom to him. "You'll be safe here."

Mom took one look at Granny and stepped out of the line. She pulled the basket out behind her.

"She's a little confused," the man said, and left us all. I wondered if he'd still be able to get the hoe he'd been looking at for the blue-light-special price.

"Oh, Sarah," Granny said. She started crying all

over again. The people in line stared at us. "I'm so confused."

"I'm here for you, Mother," Mom said, and she wrapped her arms around Granny and rocked her back and forth, the way she used to rock me when I was younger and afraid. "You took care of me and I promise I'll take care of you." Mom loosened her grip around Granny and we started toward the checkout lines, leaving the basket of layaway stuff, to pay for the candy and snacks.

Chapter Twenty-one

Private Journal of Elyse Donaldson, World-class Writer. Ideas so far: To write everything that's ever happened to me that was embarrassing, starting with when I fell down in first grade and showed my underwear and ending with Granny eating all the stock off the shelves in K Mart I wonder—Just how does Granny feel?

daffodil

For about a week Granny had what Mom called a "bad spell." When she wasn't forgetting everything, including who all of us were, she was sad or crying. She even started wishing again that she could die so she could be with Granddaddy.

"Don't be saying that, Granny," I said when she wished it for what seemed like the hundredth time.

"But, Elyse. I feel so alone. What's the use of going on?" Granny was sitting in the rocker.

"You're not alone, Granny," I said. I went up to her and put my arms around her middle. I rested my head in her lap. "You have me and Jordyn and Mom, Granny. And Aunt Maggie, too. We want you with us." Yes, Granny was weird sometimes but I couldn't stand the thought of losing her. I liked having her around. I liked loving her.

"Even when I forget? You want me even when I forget?"

I was startled by the question. I hadn't known she knew. I looked into her eyes.

"I know I'm losing time and memories," Granny said. "I've known for a while that strange things were happening to my mind."

"I want you no matter what you forget," I said, and I laid my head in her lap again. After a few seconds she rubbed my hair, her fingers tapping my head with light thumping noises.

"I love you, Elyse," Granny said. "No matter what, I love you. If I forget that, you remind me. If I forget that, you remember."

I nodded my head in her lap. "Okay, Granny," I whispered. Tears came up hot in my eyes and I swore to myself I'd never forget this moment with her.

We went for walks during the good times that week. We watched Mr. Clark till under his garden and plant some winter vegetables. We talked about when Granny was a little girl and what she remembered about me when I was a baby.

"I'm going to miss these," Granny said, spreading her fingers wide, holding her hands palm up. We were walking to the corner market to get chocolate Premium Creamies, my favorite ice cream bar. I was planning on having two.

"Miss what?" I asked Granny, thinking she meant the ice cream. "We can get them anytime we want. We only live a few blocks from the store."

"No, Elyse," Granny said, and she laughed a little. "I'm fighting an unfair battle. I was talking about missing these memories. About missing you and your mom and your sister. And Granddaddy. And my own mother and father. And Addie."

"Do you remember what Dr. Brackenbury said?" I asked. "He said you're getting better. I heard it with my own two ears."

Granny didn't say anything.

I'd kind of known Granny was forgetting, but I had never realized that she was slowly losing her past, too. It was a scary thought and it made me shiver.

"Sometimes I forget where my clothes came from. Take this shirt, for example. Yesterday I couldn't remember where I'd gotten it. This morning I saw it hanging on the back of the chair in your room and I knew it had been a present from your granddaddy. He bought this for me the last Christmas before he died."

She fingered a button on the creamy-colored shirt.

"I loved him," she said. "No, I love him."

I took Granny's hand and we walked the rest of the

180

way to the market without speaking. The sun burned down hot and I wondered about getting old myself. How would I look, wrinkled? How would I act with my friends dying? What would I do if people treated me badly?

In the store, digging through the freezer, I decided I would never get old. I would die at a ripe *young* age. I would only be a burden if I chose to be one. I would keep my home freezer stocked with chocolate Premium Creamies. I would write with one hand and eat ice cream with the other.

Walking out the door, I ran smack into Caleb. His face looked pimply and gross up so close.

"Yuck," I said without meaning to.

"You got a problem?" Caleb said, his breath warm and oniony on my face.

"Yes, I do have a problem," I said. "It's you, pizza face."

I had read that line in a book, or seen it in a movie, I couldn't remember which. I also couldn't remember what had happened to the person who called the other person pizza face. I hoped it wasn't too violent.

Patrick shoved past me into the store. I was pretty sure he hadn't heard what I said. Caleb still looked at me, though, his eyes full of hate, his face so red I bet it hurt. The glass door closed between us. An ad selling chicken blocked him from my view.

"Hurry, Granny," I said, now that we were outside. I unwrapped my ice cream and began to lick it. It didn't taste as good as usual, probably because I was getting ready to die. And young, like I had wished. "Let's get on home. I think I've made myself a problem."

Then I stopped. Maybe it was what had happened to Mr. Clark's garden that gave me courage. Maybe it was thinking about getting old and not being able to fight back. "I'm not going to run." I said this aloud.

"Oh, that's good, Elyse," Granny said. "I don't think I could run either."

"We'll walk like nothing's going to happen," I said. My heart started pounding. The sun shone bright in my eyes and my hand felt cool where the ice cream was melting onto me.

I heard the bell as the store's door swung open and closed. I heard Patrick laugh, then say, "Let's go get her." Caleb cursed an answer. It made my heart thump even harder. I wanted to run, fast. It took all my energy not to burst into the fastest sprint known to girlkind.

They jumped on their bikes and whizzed past, circling when they realized we were still so close to the store.

They stopped on their bikes and Caleb yelled.

The sun made me squint. Oh, how I wished I was

strong, like Popeye, with huge inflatable arms. I'd eat my can of spinach and saunter over to Patrick and Caleb. I'd give them what for.

"Leave me alone," I said, and my voice came out louder than I expected it to. "Quit picking on me or you're gonna be sorry." I pointed my Premium Creamie at them both. Chocolate dripped off the end.

Caleb laughed. "And what do you think you're going to do about it?"

He had a good point. I had no idea. Still, I said, "You won't push me around anymore."

"Will you hit me with that ice cream?" Patrick asked, drawing his hands up under his chin, pretending he was afraid.

"I guess you'll have to try your luck," I said, knowing full well I'd never waste good ice cream on him.

Patrick got off his bike then and sauntered to where Granny and I stood. He pushed me hard on the chest and I stumbled back, almost falling to the ground.

"No boobs," he said. Caleb laughed again.

"Come on, Elyse," Granny said. I could tell by her voice that she was worried. "I want to go home."

"Come on, Enema," Patrick imitated in a high, quivery voice. "Take me home and change my Depends diaper."

Thoughts ran through my head. Would Patrick and Caleb try to hurt me? Or worse yet, would they try and hurt Granny? We had to get out of here. I took Granny's thin hand in my own. I could feel sticky ice cream squishing between our palms.

"Oh bee-you-tee-full for spacious skies," I sang at the top of my lungs.

"Elyse?" Granny asked.

"Sing, Granny," I said. "Sing with me."

"For amber waves of grain." Granny's voice was weak but she sang with me. I started marching, pulling my grandmother along beside me.

Caleb and Patrick drove crazy-eight circles all around us, saying mean things, pretending to run into us.

I was glad that Bruce A.'s house was closer than mine was. I could make it there. I knew I could, even if I had to carry Granny on my back.

Caleb and Patrick followed us all the way to Bruce A.'s place. Granny sang with me the whole time. The walk seemed to take forever, but at last we were in Bruce A.'s front yard. Still, Caleb and Patrick yelled at us. So loud, in fact, that I didn't even have to knock on the door.

Mrs. A. opened it wide for Granny and me. "Are they bothering you?" she asked.

I nodded.

Caleb and Patrick sped off.

184

"Come in," Mrs. A. said. "What were they doing to you? Let me get Bruce. He's upstairs. I can't believe they'd harass you like that. Bruce, you have company. Is this your grandmother, Elyse? Would you like something to eat or drink? Sit here, if you want. I sure am sorry things aren't too neat . . ."

Bruce A. came pounding down the stairs. "Hi, Elyse. What's going on?"

"It's Patrick and Caleb," I said.

Bruce A. moved close to me. "What now?"

I told Bruce A. the story. "I wanted to knock their heads off," I said. "If I had had a big stick . . ."

Bruce A. sat down to think. "You can't fight them that way, Elyse. Those two will always win if you use muscle."

"Not if I was Anna-Leigh. She sure can shut them up."

"And she got into a lot of trouble."

"I didn't know that," I said.

"Her father was really angry."

"Well, you're right," I said. "But what can I do? First me, then Mr. Clark and now my grandmother."

"There's got to be something," Bruce A. said, and he patted the sofa so I could sit down next to him and we could think together.

———

I'd like to say that I wrote the article all by myself, but that's not true. Bruce A. helped. We left out an article Bruce A. had done on going back to school ("I can run it in the next issue if I want," he told me) and had ours ready before passing-out time for the next *Northwest Orem Gazette*. Anna-Leigh even did a drawing of Mr. Clark's garden before it was destroyed, a pen-and-ink one that almost looked like a photograph, it was so good.

On Sunday, even before the sun was up, I had all my papers passed out. When I finished doing my section of the neighborhood, I went back and helped Anna-Leigh pass out her papers. I made sure that there was one under a windshield wiper of each car at Caleb's and Patrick's houses. Then I went home and, sitting at the breakfast table with my whole family, read the front-page article out loud to them.

" 'Patrick Powers and Caleb Norris . . . Bullies or Heroes?' It's in big print," I said, interrupting the reading. "See? And right smack dab on the front page." *Smack dab* is something Mr. Clark always says. I like the way it sounds. When I finally get my book going I'll have a character who says *smack dab*.

"Read it," said Jordyn. "No more interruptions."

"Okay," I said. I cleared my throat. Mom sat forward, listening. I couldn't help but grin with pleasure.

186

" 'Patrick Powers and Caleb Norris . . . Bullies or Heroes? Elyse Donaldson.' " I grinned again at my family.

"Go on," Jordyn said.

I did.

Every year, as soon as the winter snows have melted and the last frost has passed, Mr. Alfred Clark begins to plant his garden. He has spent weeks getting ready for this time. He has started his plants, too many for us to name them all, from seed in a little hothouse in his basement. He has mulched the garden ground and prepared the soil for planting. He has drawn out plans that will best benefit his yard and the crops he intends to plant.

How many families are there in our little neighborhood who have tasted the tomatoes, peppers, onions and broccoli that Mr. Clark hands out at the end of the growing season? Who hasn't walked past this neighborhood garden and seen the corn growing near the back fence and the melons and pumpkins waiting to be picked? Mr. Clark's garden is a yearly event that represents the peace of our neighborhood.

Or does it?

This news reporter is here to let our peaceful

187

neighborhood know that there will be no vegetables this year. Not long ago, Caleb Norris and Patrick Powers destroyed Alfred Clark's garden in an act of vandalism. Every plant was broken. Nothing survived. And there was even an eyewitness to the destruction.

There are many who have been bothered by these two neighborhood bullies. Do we make Norris and Powers heroes by letting this abuse continue? Or do we take matters into our own hands and stop the crime on our streets?

How do we stop what is going on? Write your congressman, write the mayor, write these two vandals' parents. Let them all know we mean business.

Mr. Clark's garden can't be brought back this year. It's gone to us all. But there is next year.

And with it, the promise of peace.

I looked up at my mother and sister.

"Wow," said Mom. "Did you really write that article, Elyse?"

"Yeah," I said. "I did most of it. Bruce A. helped a little."

"You're a pretty good writer," Jordyn said. I could tell she was impressed.

"Yeah," I said, ducking my head.

"Very dramatic," said Mom.

"Will you write the letters?" I asked. "I was serious about that. Maybe if there was enough response . . ."

"I'll do it," said Jordyn. She looked at Mom.

"We'll both do it," said Mom. "I know your grandmother was pretty upset about Alfred's garden. And the way they picked on you. . . . I think a letter to those two boys' parents would be helpful."

"I don't know if it will help. We'll just have to see."

"I do have one question," said Mom.

"What?" I asked.

"Who was the eyewitness? You, Elyse?"

"No, Mom. It was Nosy Nikki. She saw Patrick and Caleb out there, but she couldn't tell what they were doing because it was still kind of early."

"So how did you find out that piece of information?" Jordyn asked.

"I hoped that maybe she had been her true self and was up early. You know how she's always complaining about the fact that she can't sleep. Bruce A. and I went over and asked her if she knew anything. She told us she saw what was going on, even though she didn't know exactly what happened until later."

"Deductive newspaper work," said Mom. "Good for you." She stood up. "Well, I'm expecting Michael anytime. He's going to help me with some things that need to be fixed around here. Maybe we can go out for Chinese food later on."

"Great," said Jordyn.

Mom stopped at the kitchen door. "Hey, Elyse," she said. "I am giving you permission to hold Bruce A.'s hand anytime you want. He's a bright boy. And he helped you out. That's good."

"He's held your hand?" Jordyn asked, her voice all silly sounding. "And why didn't you tell me?"

"They're practically engaged," Mom said.

"Engaged?" Jordyn said. It was a shriek.

"Business," I said. And I hid my face behind my newspaper.

Chapter Twenty-two

Private Journal of Elyse Donaldson, World-class Writer. Ideas so far: School starting, Granny moving, Michael Lauret becoming friends with the family   Things are changing faster than I can think.

rose quartz

Three days before school started, we moved Granny into Aspen Manor. Dr. Lauret helped again and Aunt Maggie came down, but she didn't bring Jared with her because they weren't seeing eye to eye and he had to work, anyway.

Things weren't so cheerful this move. In fact, it was awful. I begged Mom not to do it, even though in my head I knew it was the right thing.

"Please, Mom," I said, "let Granny stay with us." We had just made up Granny's own bed in room 18. I stood near the four-poster, touching the quilt, a crazy quilt that ran wild with color.

"Oh, Elyse," Mom said. "This is the way it's going to have to be. I have to work. If I could stay home with Mother, you know I would."

Granny sat in her rocker, trying to cheer everyone up by telling old knock-knock jokes. Aunt Maggie unpacked Granny's clothes and Jordyn hung photographs on the walls. Dr. Lauret moved small pieces of Granny's favorite furniture into the room.

"Why did Dad have to die?" I asked suddenly, and a little too loud. Everyone stopped what they were doing and looked at me. "If he was here, Granny could stay with us forever," I screeched. The tears in my voice were threatening to break free. "Why did he have to die?" I started crying then and fell on Granny's bed.

"Honey," Mom said, and she flopped on the bed beside me. "Shhh," she whispered.

"Don't cry," Jordyn said.

"First Dad, then Granddaddy and now Granny," I wailed. I seemed to have lost all control.

"I'll be right back," Dr. Lauret said. And he excused himself from the room. Maybe my talking about Dad made him uncomfortable. Or maybe he thought I needed to be alone with my family. I have to admit, he really is a nice guy.

"I want Granny to stay with us."

"She can't, honey," Mom said. "It's not possible."

Aunt Maggie moved over to the bed, too, and then Jordyn. I could feel them all gathered around me.

"You can see her anytime you want," Aunt Maggie said.

"I know," I said.

"And you can have your own room back," Granny said.

I looked up then and burst into new tears, painful tears that seemed to start in my heart and work their way out my eyes.

"I don't want my room back. I want you, Granny." I fell onto Mom, wrapping my arms around her neck and burying my head on her shoulder.

Somebody came to the door but I didn't know who it was because I didn't look up. The bed jiggled and I imagined Mom waving the watcher away.

"She's only going to get worse," Mom whispered.

"No," I said. "Dr. Brackenbury said she was getting better."

"What?" Mom and Aunt Maggie said the word at the same time, almost in the same tone.

I sat up, heaving with my tears. "You remember, don't you, Granny? The day I went with you for your checkup. Dr. Brackenbury said you were doing a good job, Mom. That Granny was getting better."

Mom looked at Aunt Maggie over my head. I heard Jordyn clear her throat. "You remember, don't you, Granny?" My voice was pleading. If she ever remembered anything, I needed it to be this.

My grandmother didn't say anything. She just rocked, her chair making a funny squeaking sound on the terrazzo floor.

"I think you misunderstood, Elyse," Mom said.

I shook my head. "No, I heard him. He said—"

Aunt Maggie leaned close to me. "She's not getting better."

"He said—"

"She's not getting better." It was Mom this time.

And then it hit me hard in the chest, harder than anything Caleb or Patrick had ever done to me. My grandmother was slipping away and I couldn't stop it. I had never thought of it before. I mean *really* thought of it. Eventually, Granny wouldn't remember me at all. The thought broke my heart right in two. The thought made me cringe. The thought made me cry out in pain.

I pushed myself away from Mom and looked her right in the eyes. "She's never getting better," I said. I began to cry again. "I can't stand it. The pain's all right here in my heart. It really hurts. Oh, Granny, Granny."

My voice wailed up. Jordyn closed the door. It shut with a click.

"Granny," I said. "Oh, Granny." Losing my grandmother this way was as bad as when Granddaddy had died straight out.

Mom scooped me up into her arms and rocked me gently. But the sadness stayed.

I heard Jordyn start to cry too.

"Ow," I said. "Ow."

"Elyse," said Granny. She had moved close to me. I felt her hand on my back, warm and a little bony. "Elyse, I have lived a wonderful life."

Her words made me cry all the harder.

"I have had so many wonderful things happen to me. And to see how much you love me now, what more could a grandmother ask?"

Mom sniffed and I knew she was crying too, along with me and Jordyn.

Granny squeezed in between Aunt Maggie and me until she was nearly on my lap.

"Do you remember what I said to you?"

I turned and looked at my grandmother, so tiny and frail and sweet looking. "No," I said.

"It wasn't that long ago," Granny said. "I told you to always remember that I love you. No matter what happens. Do you remember that?"

"Yes ma'am," I said, nodding and wiping at tears that refused to stop running down my face.

"And what else did I say?" Granny reached out for me and smoothed the wetness from one cheek.

"You said for me to remember that, even if you forget it."

"And will you? Elyse, you have to keep my memories for me, and pass them on to your own children. Can you do that?"

I nodded again, my heart not hurting quite so much. I would remember Granny for as long as I lived. I would never forget.

Chapter Twenty-three

Mom was true to her word. Every day after school Jordyn and I picked up Granny from Aspen Manor. Even when she wasn't herself.

And when she was, Granny and I talked. She told me about being a little girl in Utah in the olden days. She talked about Mom and Aunt Maggie being young and funny. She told me about my father and about me, too. I didn't have time for a journal anymore. Instead I wrote down the things Granny said. I saved every word, sometimes taping her, sometimes borrowing Michael's video camera. (Dr. Lauret insists I call him Michael now, even when I go into the office he shares with my orthodontist and get my braces worked on. I hope he won't insist on my calling him Dad anytime soon.)

And lots of times, when she was herself, Granny reminded me she loved me.

One evening, while I was doing the dishes with Jordyn, talking about school and how I had a pretty good English teacher, a whooping noise sounded from my room. The room that had been mine, then Granny's and was now mine again. The sunroom was free of my mess, much to Mom's relief.

"Whoa there, fish, whoa."

"Oh no," I said. I laughed a little.

"Help!" Granny called, startling me. "Help! I'm trapped." Her voice was thin, not the same fish-calling voice of the moment before.

"What now?" Mom asked the ceiling.

"Help," Granny called again. "I can't get loose. I'm drowning. Let go, fish. Let go."

Mom leaped from the table and took off running.

"Help!"

Drowning, I thought. *There's no water except in the bathroom. The bathroom?* Fear flooded my heart and I followed Jordyn, who had chased right after Mom.

"Elyse," Mom said. She was in my bedroom.

"What?" I asked, and then, "Oh."

Granny sat waist deep in the clothes pile I had in the corner. She was so twisted up and tangled that she couldn't even move. Only her hands flapped. There was a blue-striped sock on her head.

"Fish," Granny said, holding the palms of her hands out.

I began to laugh. I tried not to. I held it in as long as I could, and when the laughter came out it was a giant-sounding thing.

"This isn't funny, Elyse," Mom said. "Help me loosen her."

"Okay," I said, and I smothered the laugh.

"Jordyn," Mom said. "Come and help me untangle your grandmother."

"Help," Granny called. "I'm drowning. Fish."

Jordyn moved to Mom's side and they began to pull the clothes off Granny. She wore some of them, a pair of blue jeans on her arm, a shirt wrapped around her upper body. But mostly she was just tangled up.

At last Granny was free. She sat on the pile of clothes on my floor, a comical expression on her face, the sock still on her head.

I smiled at her, then took the sock off. I knelt in front of her and put my arms around her neck. After a moment Mom put her arms around Granny and me, and then Jordyn came close to us and hugged everybody too.

"I love you, Granny," I said.

"I love you too, Addie," she said.

———

In seventh-grade English, Mrs. Markham talked to us about correct grammar. She talked to us about writing a journal and keeping tabs on our feelings. She asked our opinions and listened to them. She talked to us about our home lives and told us how there are stories in our families.

That's the truth, I thought. Then she asked us to write a paper about what we knew well: living at home.

In my old room, I looked through my summer journal. Nearly everything I had written that still mattered was about Granny. I was glad.

After a lot of thinking, I titled my paper "Granny, Forever in the Donaldson Home." It was corny, I knew, but I meant it. It was also long—the paper, I mean—and though I'd never admit it out loud, heartfelt, too.

When I got my paper back there was a note at the end of it written in red ink. It said:

Elyse. You have some originality. I look forward to seeing your writing. Mrs. Earl told me all about you and what a joy you would be to have in class. She was right. A+

> *Mrs. M.*

An A+ on my first seventh-grade writing project. I folded the paper carefully and put it in my English notebook. I would save this note forever. Mrs. Earl had said nice things about me to another teacher. She had told me I was a world-class writer. I think she was right.

I thought about the novel I had been going to write all summer. It seemed it was time to start on it again. Maybe even using paper and pencil this time. Or our ancient typewriter, if I got a ribbon.

Maybe, I thought, maybe I would write about Granny.

Author's Note

Currently in America, about four million people have been diagnosed with Alzheimer's disease. The symptoms appear gradually and may include memory loss, confusion about time and place, language problems (such as trouble remembering words), and changes in personality. Once a person is diagnosed with AD, he or she may live with the disease as long as twenty-five years. As time passes, the patient will have more and more trouble remembering and will eventually end up being cared for by someone else. Many patients are like Elyse's granny in this book: They live at home, not in a nursing home. If you have a friend or relative who has AD, what can you do?

Be loving and kind to that person. Although there is no cure for AD yet, a calm and orderly environment can help. Physical exercise and social activity are important, too. If you know someone with AD, have hope. Even now there are medications that, if given early in the disease, can slow the degeneration process. Maybe someday there will be a cure. Maybe you will find it.

Carol Lynch Williams